Dr. Emily Berthoff was as gorgeous as ever.

Emily raised her eyes and met Kevin's. Her demure smile seemed to hold a touch of sadness and the air whooshed from his lungs, leaving him with a burning need for oxygen.

He studied her intently, remembering.... Suddenly her hunter-green dress faded to white, a veil covered her face and her smile was full of love.... Kevin furiously blinked the dream away.

"Why didn't you tell me Emily was coming?" Kevin asked.

His best friend, Bryan, looked unconvincingly baffled. "Did I forget to mention that?"

"Yeah, I'd say you forgot to mention that!" Kevin mocked.

"A lot has changed in seven years."

Kevin scowled at his friend. "Eight. And yeah, a lot has changed. I've just made a bid that will put my entire business at stake, and I don't need some woman turning my life around to fit her agenda."

"I wouldn't exactly call your ex-fiancée *some woman.*"

Books by Carol Steward

Love Inspired

There Comes a Season #27
Her Kind of Hero #56
Second Time Around #92

CAROL STEWARD

lives with her hero/husband of twenty years and three teenage children in Greeley, Colorado. When she isn't busy caring for preschoolers in her home, she keeps busy with the activities of her daughter and two sons, and with volunteer work for various organizations. A retired cake decorator, Carol enjoys camping, restoring antiques, tole-painting, needlework, gardening, traveling, sewing and collecting Noah's Ark items.

She loves to hear from readers. You may write to her at Carol Steward P.O. Box 5021 Greeley, CO 80631-0021.

Second Time Around

Carol Steward

Published by Steeple Hill Books™

STEEPLE HILL BOOKS

ISBN 0-373-87098-1

SECOND TIME AROUND

This edition published by arrangement with Steeple Hill Books.

Visit us at www.steeplehill.com

Printed in U.S.A.

Two are better than one, because they have a good reward for their toil. For if they fall, one will lift up his fellow; but woe to him who is alone when he falls and has not another to lift him up....
A threefold cord is not quickly broken.

—Ecclesiastes 4:9-10, 12

For my mother, Phillis Bohannan, for teaching me never to give up. Thanks, Mom.

Acknowledgments:

To Robin and Michelle for your inspiration even before God introduced us.

Many thanks to Marty, Deb and Bette for your expertise and continued support.

Chapter One

From the parlor, building contractor Kevin MacIntyre heard the church bells outside announcing the celebration. He ran a finger inside his shirt collar, suddenly feeling as stuffed as insulation between two-by-four studs. Why the suit bothered him today, he hadn't a clue. He wasn't the type to shy away from formal occasions. In fact, he typically enjoyed them. He guessed it was because his best friend was making the long-awaited trip to the altar, and Kevin had yet to find Miss Perfect. *With all the hours I'm putting in at work, I don't have time for anyone else, anyway. What do I care?*

Kevin picked up a miniature plastic football and tossed it to the groom. The music began softly, then grew louder and faster. Kevin opened the door to the chapel and peeked out to see if it was time for them to take their places. The usher escorted the beautiful guest down the aisle on his arm. Dr. Emily Berthoff was as gorgeous as ever.

Emily raised her eyes and met Kevin's. Her demure smile seemed to hold a touch of sadness, and the air whooshed from his lungs, leaving him with a burning need for oxygen.

He studied her intently, remembering... Suddenly, her hunter-green dress faded to white, a veil covered her face, and her smile was full of love.... Kevin furiously blinked the dream away. No longer concerned with starting any wedding, he pushed the door closed. "Why didn't you tell me Emily was coming?"

The groom looked unconvincingly baffled. "Did I forget to mention that?" Bryan threw the football back across the room, the ball hitting Kevin in the stomach before dropping to the floor.

"Yeah, I'd say you forgot to mention that!" Kevin mocked.

Bryan followed his chortling toddler across the room to get the toy, and the two embraced in a growling hug. "Just be glad Barb is feeling better. Laura was going to ask Emily to stand in as the maid of honor."

Kevin straightened his suit, then combed the unruly waves of hair back into place with his fingers. "Laura's trying to get even with me, isn't she? Your future wife has a warped sense of humor."

Bryan chuckled.

Jacob handed Kevin the football. He picked the toddler up and tossed Bryan the ball. "Go tackle your dad," Kevin whispered into Jacob's ear as he set the boy down. Then Kevin watched with envy as his best friend and son played together, casually waiting for Pastor Mike to come for them. *I'm going to miss having Jacob around.*

"She's a romantic. Thinks you and Emily should

give it another try.'' Bryan checked his watch, stuffed the toys into a baby-size backpack, then pulled his suit jacket on. ''You've got to admit, Emily is still available—not to mention as beautiful as always.''

''Even if I did admit it, it doesn't mean anything.'' Kevin had chased away memories of Emily Berthoff long ago. Moved on with his life. Pursued his dreams and was on the verge of making them come true. And she was no longer a part of the plan.

''Maybe Laura's right, Kevin. A lot has changed in seven years.''

He scowled at his friend. ''Eight. It was the year the Buffs beat Nebraska. Yeah, a lot has changed. I've just made a bid that will put my entire business at stake, not to mention the risk I've let you take on this investment. I want to pay you back as soon as possible. I don't need some woman turning my life around to fit her agenda.''

Bryan smoothed his son's tiny vest, while obviously trying to wipe the smirk from his own lips. ''I wouldn't exactly call your ex-fiancée *some woman.* That in itself tells me how you feel about her.''

''Wait just a minute here! Don't go assuming anything. Seeing her here surprised me. That's all.'' Kevin checked his pocket for Laura's wedding ring, wishing Bryan would let the issue die, just as his and Emily's relationship had died. ''It's been too long to care what the doctor does. She made her choices.''

Until he had unexpectedly run into Emily in Laura's hospital room two months ago, he'd successfully erased the enchanting woman from existence. Since then, unmanageable thoughts plagued his mind with reruns of the years they had been together: dreams of a family, of traveling across the country together, of waking up to one another—

Bryan's somber voice interrupted him again. "Put the show aside, Kevin. I know it hurts. You're not going to like this, but I'm going to say it anyway...."

Kevin wanted to walk out of the room in the worst way. He didn't need Mr. Happy here to throw his own words back in his face. Problem was, on the other side of that door was a chapel full of smiling loved ones ready to celebrate "happily ever after." There was no escaping. No matter how desperately he wanted to leave, he couldn't do that to his best friend. Not today.

"It's time you put the past behind you and looked at your future. And Emily's as good a place as any to start."

Kevin started to say something, and was politely told to wait his turn. The echo of his own words reverberated in his ears. He couldn't believe it had been little more than a year since he'd used that same line on Bryan. "Just because it worked for you, don't count on it changing my life."

"Come on, Jacob, hold still." Bryan stood his son on the sofa and straightened the toddler's tiny bow tie. Returning his attention to Kevin, he added, "You never stopped caring for her. If it hadn't been for your dad, you probably would have gone after her then."

Kevin tugged on the knot of his own necktie, certain it was getting tighter by the minute. "Drop the subject, Bryan."

Bryan stepped in front of him and looked him in the eye as he readjusted the silk strip around Kevin's neck. "That's why you haven't stayed with any other woman. You only have feelings for the one who walked away. Swallow your pride, Kevin. Talk to her. You owe it to both of you to settle it, once and for all."

"Forget it." There was nothing more to say. He didn't want to see, let alone talk to Emily Berthoff, M.D., again. Not because it might rekindle the fire, but because his fire had never gone out.

The tall oak door opened and a middle-aged pastor with a receding hairline nodded. "Morning, Kevin. You ready, Bryan?"

"Thought you'd never get here." Still staring Kevin in the eye, Bryan waggled his eyebrows. "Best day of my life."

Kevin walked behind Pastor Mike and the groom into the small chapel filled with candles and flowers and smiling faces. He watched the bride's father present Laura to Bryan. Their gazes were fixed on each other and love radiated between them.

"We are gathered here to celebrate the union of Laura Bates and Bryan Beaumont...."

Even in his sulking mood, he couldn't help but feel the happiness choke out the bitterness. He laughed at Laura's youngest son, who was fidgeting with his suit. Kevin lowered his eyebrows and shook his head slightly until the boy stopped. Bryan was going to have his hands full. In just over a year he'd gone from no children to four; from married, to widowed, to honeymooner. *You have my best wishes, friend.*

The soloist sang about love that never ended, and Kevin felt the noose around his neck slip another notch tighter.

He found Emily instinctively, yet stubbornly

turned away. With beautiful red hair and a bright smile, she had always stood out in a crowd. Always would. His mind drifted to bitter memories of that day, a month before their wedding, when Emily had announced she'd unexpectedly been accepted into a prestigious medical school—across the country. The day when the very foundation of his dreams had crumbled like bad concrete.

Though they had known there was a remote possibility she'd be accepted at Johns Hopkins, they'd made their plans based upon her attending medical school in-state.

Time was supposed to heal all wounds, so the saying went. It hadn't worked in eight years, and he doubted it ever would. In that respect, Bryan was right; there would be no one for him, because the only woman he'd ever loved had walked away.

Bryan nudged his hand, and Kevin realized he had missed his cue. He reached into his pocket and pulled out Laura's wedding ring. He glanced at the bride, who had the smug look of a woman who already had a scheme in mind.

"Relax, your time will come," Bryan whispered as Kevin handed him the ring.

"Not a chance." He was supposed to be the one calming the groom. Not the other way around.

In what seemed like minutes, Laura and Bryan were pronounced husband and wife, and the two were joined by four rambunctious children for a walk down the aisle. Kevin waited for the music to change, then followed, trying to ignore the striking woman in the third pew.

Two hours later, the celebration was winding down. Kevin must have talked to every person in the reception hall, except the pretty doctor. Somehow they had managed to miss one another. He supposed he had the pastor to thank for keeping Emily company. Glancing quickly around the room, he consoled himself with the realization that she had left first, without making any effort to talk to him.

He backed through the arched doorway and spun around, ready to make a quick escape up the stairs, out the door, and away from this lousy trip into his unpleasant past.

"They're perfect for each other, aren't they?"

Kevin stumbled up the step as he turned toward the all-too-familiar voice. The slick sole of his shoes on the metal edge sent him sprawling across the stairs. Clenching his jaw to swallow the cry, a deep rumble vibrated against his vocal cords.

"Kevin! Are you okay?"

He groaned. "Why in blazes are you hiding in here?"

"I was paged and needed a quieter place to phone the hospital." Emily extended her hand to help him up. "I didn't mean to startle you."

He brushed her hand aside, stunned by the sincerity of her remark. After all this time, he wasn't going to let Emily get to him. "I'll be fine, thanks for the concern, Doc."

Children squealed and raced past them across the room in a raucous game of kissing tag. A look of admiration softened Emily's green eyes. She tipped her head toward the chaos. "Who would have pictured Bryan as a father of four? Laura is so much better for him than Andrea, isn't she?"

Tearing his gaze from Emily, Kevin looked at the

bride and groom. "Like night and day. It took a while, but I finally got through to them."

She flipped her cellular phone closed and put it into a compact purse, her tone turning cold. "How generous of you. Must have been the jealousy routine. You were always so good at that one."

He studied her as she concentrated on the newlyweds. Emily's full lips turned into a smile that crinkled the corners of her eyes as she watched the giddy couple behind the tiered cake. Kevin closed his eyes, wishing after all these years he could forget how wonderful it was to hold her in his arms and kiss the soft fullness of her lips. *Don't be a fool. Emily is off-limits.*

Wishing she didn't still have the power to make his heart skip a beat, Kevin tugged the knot of his tie loose. "So that was it. Your mother convinced you that all men were like your father, huh? And all this time, I thought it was medical school that lured you away."

The smile disappeared and her eyebrows arched up. "And apparently you still think I should have given up the opportunity of a lifetime to follow *your* dreams. I'm relieved to know I made the right decision." Emily turned to leave.

Following her through the doorway, he grabbed her hand. "We can both be happy you realized your career was more important than a family *before* it was too late."

"How dare you," she countered in a broken voice.

Kevin stepped in front of her, deliberately blocking her view of the festivities.

"Sorry if I hit a nerve."

"You're not a bit sorry."

"Oh, there you're wrong, Doc. There are a lot of things I'm sorry about." He could never forget the tailspin her announcement had sent him into. It had short-circuited his very existence. "But I guess you're not interested in hearing all of that, are you?"

Emily's green eyes widened like those of a cat ready to pounce, yet she remained silent.

He let go of her silky-soft hand, and she stepped back as if giving up without a battle. He should have remembered, their arguments always made her nervous, the tragic remains of a broken home. She lowered her head, and he could no longer see her face through her veil of red curls.

She glanced at him, then away.

Was that a tear? He yanked his tie from around his neck, unfastened the top button, and dragged in a quick breath, inhaling the sweet smell of her perfume. The last thing he had expected was that she would cry.

She cleared her throat and looked at the tie dangling in his hand. "You know, Kevin, I didn't notice you trying to contact me, either. The final decision was yours," she said with renewed determination.

Kevin backed away. The old Emily wouldn't have made a scene. Especially not in a public place. "There *was* no choice," he said quietly.

"No choice?" she repeated. "Funny, isn't it? You're here in Springville *now*. Yet the family's business that couldn't manage without you then, isn't."

He wondered if he should tell her why, then decided against it. It was best to leave things as they were. She was the one who had walked away. Let her think what she wanted. Their future was long gone.

Raw pain glimmered in her misty eyes.

He felt the rapid beating in his chest and wondered if he could have been wrong, then immediately pushed the thought away. He had his business to consider now.

"Fate is a funny thing for sure." He studied her puzzled look and laughed softly. Forcing the question away, he added, "Who would ever have guessed we'd wind up here together?"

"'Together' is a bit presumptuous, isn't it? We've managed to avoid each other up until now—that shouldn't be too difficult to continue. After all, we have no reason to see each other." She walked into the main reception hall, stopped by the crowd gathering around the bride and groom.

He wanted to tell her he was bidding for the project on her clinic, but couldn't risk placing her in an awkward situation. And because the bids were closed, he didn't want to jeopardize his chances, either. *This is business. Strictly business.*

Crowding in behind her, he whispered in her ear. "Face it, Emily, we will see each other. I assure you." He chuckled, then quickly chastised himself for entertaining the thought of walking into her office on a daily basis to prove his point. *You're playing with fire, Kevin,* said a voice inside him.

She spun around.

Gazing into her eyes was a mistake. He forced away the sudden image of kissing her and putting that wedding ring on her finger—for good this time.

He turned to see what the commotion was behind him, just in time to see the bouquet bounce like a volleyball from one female to the next...and into his own hands. Cheers and laughs filled the room.

"Sorry, ladies, I'm out of the running." He shrugged his shoulders and smiled, then tossed the bouquet back into the air.

Emily had sidestepped her way past him and was escaping into the crowd. But the bridal bouquet arched toward her. Obviously surprised, Emily reached out and caught it.

She spun around and shot Kevin a cold, hard stare. Then she threw the flowers back at him, turned and ran.

Chapter Two

Emily frantically chopped the onion, tears rolling down her face. ''Who does he think he is?''

''Sounds just the same as *I* remember him.'' Her younger sister looked at the cutting board. ''Are we going to eat that onion, or drink it?''

Emily glanced at the pile of pulverized white mush. ''When did you get so picky?''

''Well, normally I wouldn't argue, but we're making salad, not stew.'' Katarina scraped the mess into the garbage disposal, rinsed the wooden slab, then walked across the kitchen, drying the cutting board with a towel. ''So Kevin still looks great, huh?''

''I didn't say anything about the way he had looked—did I?'' Emily was certain she hadn't told her sister he looked so devastatingly handsome that she had even failed to notice what color of dress the matron of honor was wearing. She didn't tell Katarina Kevin's hair was blonder than before, his skin more bronzed and his laugh even huskier. She hadn't, and she wouldn't. She didn't dare.

Katarina disappeared into the other room, but her raised voice more than made up for the distance. "You may have the M.D. behind your name, sis, but *I'm* the heart specialist." Her sister's honey-blond head momentarily peeked around the corner. "And trust me, that onion was not strong enough to warrant that river of tears."

When Katarina reappeared from the living room, soft music floated in behind her swaying body. "Maybe ocean waves will help you relax. You really do need to lighten up, sis."

Her sister was right. She was too serious. Emily pulled another onion from the hanging basket and chopped a couple of slices, then set the cutting board in front of her cheery sister. "*There* is your onion."

"Why are you mad at me?" Katarina shrugged her shoulders, hands palms up in front of her. "I didn't tell you to break your engagement with Kevin to become a doctor for my sake. In fact, if you'd asked, I'd have said you were crazy to let Kevin go. My hearing was already damaged—nothing anyone could have done, including you. The job of Savior has already been filled—in case you need another reminder."

"That's not even funny, Katarina."

"Lighten up, sis. I was joking!"

Emily's focus instantly moved to the hearing aid tucked into her sister's right ear. "Oh, Kat. I'm sorry. I don't blame you." Emily set the knife on the ceramic-tile counter and rinsed her hands, then hugged her younger sister. "No, sweetie. It wasn't just because of you. It was for families like ours who grew up without the money to get proper medical care. If you'd only had the medicine for your ear infections, you'd be fine now."

Katarina's eyes clouded, and Emily saw sudden visions of their impoverished childhood. She leaned back and tucked a stray hair behind her ear, remembering arguments she and Kevin had had regarding family finances. "I'm sorry," she whispered. "Guess I haven't let go of my past after all, have I? I hand it to God, then I yank it back. Bet He thinks it's a yo-yo by now."

Kat reached out her hand and held Emily's, her ornery smile erasing the look of hurt from her blue eyes. "I think there's one part of your past you'd better examine very carefully before letting him slip away a second time."

Emily turned her sister's head and spoke into her ear. "Is your hearing aid on?" she teased.

Katarina nodded.

"Good, because I don't want you to miss what I'm going to say. I don't care about Kevin MacIntyre." Emily tugged the unruly curls to the top of her head and fastened a barrette, then continued. "I don't wish him any harm, but...I don't need him. I am perfectly happy on my own."

"Right. I don't believe a word of it, but the time will come when you'll realize what he still means to you."

Emily watched her sister dance to the back door and pull the Victorian lace curtains closed, seemingly mocking Emily's problems. Katarina was the only sane person she knew who could switch moods as easily as turning pages on a calendar.

"I am curious," Kat continued. "How do you

plan to avoid him when both of you are friends with Laura and Bryan?"

"They'll understand." Emily placed the ivy-trimmed dishes on the antique table and added two glasses of iced tea. She thought of Kevin's promise that they would see each other again, and the seething anger started anew. "Oooh, he's so sure of himself."

Katarina didn't say anything, just smiled. The disk changed, and it wasn't long before she began humming with the music. Pretty soon, Emily heard an echo of the wedding processional behind her.

"Knock it off, Katarina."

"Mama always said your temper was because of that fiery red hair. Came from the Irish side of the family, I suppose."

Emily shook her head and rolled her eyes, remembering their childish arguments as if they were yesterday.

They continued preparing dinner in silence. Even though Katarina irritated her like only a little sister could, Emily was anxious for Kat's move to town so they could get together more often. They were the closest of the three siblings in age and in spirit.

If it hadn't been for her sister's youthful encouragement, Emily never would have made it through the broken engagement or medical school. Kat's zany sense of humor was a totally endearing quality that Emily had learned to appreciate, and had come to depend upon.

"Emily?" Her sister touched her arm.

She turned, shaking the daze away. "What?"

Kat had moved the food to the table, and now motioned for Emily to sit. In unison they bowed their heads, while Emily blessed the nourishment before them.

There was an unsettling quiet as they ate.

"Do you think Dad ever loved Mom?" After all these years, Katarina's voice echoed Emily's gnawing childhood fear.

Emily stared at her food. Would the mention of her broken engagement ever stop reminding all of them of their father? "I try not to analyze them, Kat. We both know how unforgiving Mom can be. Maybe Dad couldn't take it anymore. Maybe... Who knows?" Emily shrugged, then took a bite of chicken. She wished her sister would change the subject.

"Don't you ever wonder why he never came back to see us?"

Slurping the juice dripping from the bite of pear, Emily mumbled, "Of course I do. I doubt I'll ever get over it."

"What?" Katarina turned her head slightly, tears brimming in her bright blue eyes. Out of frustration, she combed her fingers through one side of her sporty hairstyle, as if the hair were preventing her hearing aid from working.

"I mean, there are parts of my past I can't seem to forget." The hearing aid in Katarina's ear was tiny and no longer bothered her, but it always would Emily. It was a constant reminder of why she'd gone into medicine. No matter how much she tried, Emily would never forget the pain she'd nursed her little sister through. She'd do everything possible to help prevent another child's suffering. "How do you deal with it? You're always so disgustingly cheerful."

The brightness of her sister's porcelain skin paled

and the smile dimmed. "There are still days when I'm so mad I could spit nails. Trust me."

Emily took her sister's hand and squeezed it. "I'm sure there are, Kat." Caring for Katarina and their youngest sister, Lisa, while her mother had worked two jobs had made Emily realize the importance of an education. Which was why she and Kevin had agreed to wait until she finished her bachelor's degree to get married. Then came that letter—

Her mind pulled the plug on the memory. "Hey, we're supposed to be having a good time tonight. Who brought up this maudlin subject, anyway?"

Katarina grinned. "You're right. Let's change the subject. So, tell me more about the wedding. The part without Kevin, if you'd prefer."

In between bites of chicken *cordon bleu* and salad, Emily told her everything, *excluding* the charming way Kevin had played with the kids during the reception. Remembering it made her heart swell. There he was in his tailored suit, romping around on the floor with Laura's sons so the bride and groom could enjoy the reception....

His thoughtfulness and boyish sense of humor were what had first caught her attention so many years ago. She had been sitting solemnly by herself under the golden leaves of the grand old maple tree at the college-sponsored concert, when Kevin spied her staring at him. Even from a distance, she'd seen the way he made everyone around him feel. He had a contagious laugh and a quick wit. As she blushed, he introduced himself. A few minutes later they were sharing the shade, deep in conversation and laughter.

For three years he'd courted her, throughout it all putting up with her mother's ridicule. But Emily had stayed, falling ever more deeply in love with the man her mother had predicted would love her and leave her, just as Emily's philandering father had done.

"I'm going to Lincoln next week for a show. Do you want me to take anything to Mom?" If her sister noticed Emily's distraction, she didn't mention it.

Emily welcomed the interruption.

"Mom... Oh, yeah, would you take her birthday present?"

"What did you get her? I haven't found anything yet."

"It's an airline ticket. Thought I'd take her to the mountains. Care to join us? I've borrowed Laura and Bryan's cabin for a week."

"Sounds fun. I'll check my schedule. With the move, I may have to make a last-minute decision depending on how everything is going."

"I thought I'd see if Lisa can join us, too. We'll make it a family reunion."

After catching up on the latest on Lisa and her beau, they discussed Kat's growing business and her worries of keeping up with the demand for her designer dolls.

Clearing the dishes while Katarina called her on-again-off-again boyfriend, Emily let her thoughts return to their mother's influence on the three daughters' relationships. Katarina couldn't take that final plunge into matrimony. Lisa didn't date any man long enough to fall in love.

And Emily—the broken engagement to Kevin had been enough to send the frightened child in her running as far as possible from love and commitment.

Eight years later, she was still running.

* * *

Two weeks had passed since her sister's visit, and since she'd seen Kevin. Emily walked into the church's preschool to tell the children about being a doctor. She and the teacher visited for a few minutes before a little boy from Emily's Sunday school class grabbed her hand. "Dr. Emily, come see what a tall tower I can build." She followed Ricky, welcoming the chance to visit with the little boy away from the examination room.

For the next half hour, Emily watched as Ricky played with the children. After Circle Time, they prepared for the guests to talk about their careers. A cake decorator was first, and gave each child an ornately decorated cookie to keep each busy while she turned a mound of cake into a stand-up penguin.

Emily was next. She looked at the cake and the children eagerly eating cookies. *Great, how do I top this?*

After telling the children about how much she enjoyed being a doctor, she pulled the stethoscope out of her pocket.

"Dr. Emily, can I listen to your heart?" Ricky blurted out, his raised hand flapping back and forth.

"Sure. You can each have a turn. Come up one at a time." The familiar boy with streaked brown hair jumped to his feet and nearly leaped over the kids sitting in front of him. Emily recognized most of the children, either from Sunday school or the medical clinic. Before she knew it, all the children were crowded around.

"Shh," Emily prompted. "We must be very quiet."

Ricky listened for a minute, then expertly moved the stethoscope. She wanted to cry at the extent of his knowledge of the workings of the instrument, which came from more hands-on experience than any child his age should have.

"I don't hear anything, Dr Emily." He frowned. "I think you have a broken heart."

A deep chuckle rumbled behind them. "An insightful young man."

Emily's heart raced at the sound of Kevin's voice.

The little boy's brown eyes grew larger. "Wow! There it is. It's beating as fast as Thumper's paw. 'Member, in Bambi?"

"Are you twitterpated, Dr. Emily?" a precocious little girl asked.

"Twitterpated?"

"You know, in *love.*" The little girl sighed. "Like Bambi and Faline."

Emily felt the blood rush to her cheeks. "No, I'm not. We'd better let someone else have a turn now, Ricky." She gave him a hug and watched as he ran across the room...to Kevin.

Kevin knelt down and spent several minutes in conversation with the child. From the corner of her eye, Emily watched, angry at herself for paying Kevin any attention.

The other preschoolers filed past, and Emily helped them listen to each other's hearts beating. Ricky moved back to the circle of children after giving Kevin a high-five. Then Kevin visited with a parent, while Emily finished talking with the children and gave them the disposable masks and hats.

Then she turned the stage over to Kevin. He leaned close as Emily walked past. "Any time your heart needs a jump start, let me know."

"You'd be the last person I'd call," she mumbled,

wishing she could dispel her reaction to him. Emily silently joined the parent volunteer in the back of the room. She and the other woman listened as Kevin told about the construction business, demonstrating with a toy log set.

The children were mesmerized by the rugged-looking man with the contagious smile and rumbling laugh. Other than the uncustomarily clean blue jeans, he looked every bit the brawny construction worker. A red-plaid flannel shirt over a blue T-shirt and a bright yellow hard hat completed the irresistible image. His strong hands moved the tiny logs with the same delicacy one would use to move fine china.

All the little boys proclaimed they, too, wanted to be builders after his enthusiastic description of tearing walls apart and building others. The energy in the room began to escalate.

"Why did you become a builder?" The teacher prompted the conversation back to the subject, her calming voice reminding the children to listen.

"My father was a builder, and it was something I always enjoyed. It's hard work, but I like bringing families together in a new home," he said.

It was obvious that he loved talking to the youngsters. The children drilled him with questions, and he took time to answer each one. He still had his way with kids.

Emily wondered why he hadn't married. Coming from a family with six children, he had wanted to have at least four of his own. He had chivalrously promised Emily that he'd support them all, yet that wasn't enough for Emily. She wanted a career of her own, one through which she could provide for her family, if necessary. She wasn't about to watch history repeat itself.

Emily stared critically at Kevin. Why was he here? How had he, of all people, come to be asked to speak to the preschool?

Kevin smiled lazily, then winked at her before saying goodbye to the preschoolers. She realized the desperate attempts she was making to taint her image of the only man who could touch her heart with a mere glance.

The children would be leaving soon, and this was Kevin's only chance to talk to Emily alone. As he exited the preschool room, he nodded for her to join him outside. He could see her reluctance.

"Why are you here?" she demanded as soon as the door closed behind them.

He folded his arms across his chest and smiled. "I heard there was a damsel inside with a broken heart. Thought I'd come to the rescue."

"Very funny."

He smiled. He had decided after the confusion at the wedding that he needed to find out if she was still interested—if that had been the reason for her tears. He challenged himself to make her laugh. Or at least smile. She had a beautiful smile. "Actually, I was just waiting for the rescue breathing."

Her eyes were clear as green ice. "I'm serious."

"It's obvious that hasn't changed."

Emily put her hands on her hips and waited. She had changed from the college co-ed he'd fallen in love with, he thought. Her shyness had matured to a quiet confidence, her insecurities had been replaced by a calm determination, and her wide-eyed look of fear reflected a love that hadn't died.

"Okay, the truth," he continued, hoping that reflection was wrong. "I'm working on developing a new image." He started to tell her about the bid, but she took an abrupt step toward him and flashed him a look of annoyance.

"I really would have thought you'd grow up a little in eight years." She turned and walked back inside.

"Just as I thought, you can't handle the truth," he mumbled, once she had turned the corner and disappeared from sight.

Kevin recalled Laura begging him to come talk to the preschoolers. He glanced through the narrow slat of a window into the preschool and watched as a little boy clung to the teacher, doing whatever he could to get her attention. There was no question in Kevin's mind that Laura was trying to set him and Emily up again.

"Better luck next time, lady."

Chapter Three

The conference room was filled with the aroma of gourmet coffee and glazed doughnuts. Sunlight filtered in through the broken slats of the blinds. The chief of staff addressed the doctors and board members, summarizing the top three clinic renovation proposals. At the mention of a small independent builder, Emily let out a quick gasp.

Her colleague Bob Walker leaned close. "What's wrong, Em?" he whispered. "You look like you've seen a ghost."

Ignoring him, Emily examined the different bid summaries with a sudden urgency. Why hadn't she considered this possibility earlier? Muffled voices buzzed around her. Her heart rate increased. *He wouldn't dare.*

Dr. Bob Walker pushed a note in front of her, a barely legible invitation to join him for dinner scrawled across the prescription pad. Sending him a reprimand from the corner of her eye, she scrunched the note into a tiny ball and tossed it into the trash can.

She thumbed back through the folders and, with a sudden chill of comprehension, looked again at the unbelievably low bid. Kevin was vying for this job. That's why he had been so confident he'd be seeing her again.

"Emily? What are your feelings about the bids?"

"Yes, Emily, what are you thinking?" Bob added, a mischievous glint in his eye.

Still dismayed, she cleared her throat and brushed a stray hair off her forehead. With a quick appraisal of the spreadsheets before her, it was hard to argue the obvious. "Since the project committee is behind on fund-raising, I'll admit it does make this incredibly low bid very appealing."

The other committee members nodded. Dr. Roberts agreed, adding, "With the incentives City Council is offering, I think it's critical that we make the commitment now. Sonshine Medical Clinic is finally gaining the support we need."

Emily closed the folder, suddenly aware of what the outcome of this vote could mean to her own peace of mind. No matter what happened between her and Kevin, she reminded herself, this was business. *If* the contractor was Kevin...she'd learn to deal with it when the time came. If not, her paranoia could cost both the clinic and the company bidding a very important project. She had to keep her personal turmoil out of the way.

"There isn't really any question, is there?" Dr. Walker added.

Not regarding which sealed bid to accept, maybe,

but Emily had plenty of questions, doubts and uncertainties.

The company was offering incredible upgrades that the clinic couldn't otherwise afford. How could Kevin afford to be so generous? Surely his fledgling company didn't have this kind of money to donate. And from the way he'd reacted to seeing her at Laura and Bryan's wedding, he wasn't trying to win her over again. *Surely I'm just imagining this. Kevin doesn't want to be near me any more than I want him around. He wouldn't do this.*

There was no question but that she wanted the clinic to flourish. She wanted to help their patients. And despite her and Kevin's history, she wished him every success, both personally and professionally. She just didn't like the idea of their goals being mutually dependent.

Turning her mind back to the meeting, she concentrated on the discussion. Others expressed gratitude at the upgrades, and Emily added suspiciously, "Can we trust his word on that?" The faces around the table looked puzzled by her sudden lack of enthusiasm. "It's just—I'm merely concerned that we be sure the company will follow through once it has the job in hand. Well, it does seem determined to win this bid, doesn't it? Question is, how many promises would the company make in order to get the job?"

Everyone began talking at once, and Bob leaned close. "You know something about this company, Em? I've never seen you so feisty. To be honest, I like it."

"What's wrong, Bob? Did the new receptionist break your date?" She edged away.

He smiled. "Come on, have dinner with me. No one need find out."

Emily looked around the table, then turned her head so that only Bob could hear. "I think you're making a big mistake, Bob. Your third strike with me was two receptionists and six months ago. One more, and you'll strike yourself out of the clinic, as well."

The doctor sobered, and leaned back in his chair, nonchalantly pretending he hadn't heard anything she'd said. That was fine with her. Just so he understood.

Emily let her mind wander back to Kevin as the board's discussion progressed without her.

Thirty minutes later the chief of staff spun his pen on the chipped tabletop. "I think it's obvious that number two believes in our mission. Unless there's any disagreement, I'll share our feelings with the board and let them make the announcement." All present turned and looked at Emily, anticipating another argument.

What if it's not *Kevin? Can I take that chance?* She shook her head.

As the others made their way through the conference room door, she opened the folder again, looking more carefully for some inkling of proof. Could Kevin believe in the clinic's mission? She saw no evidence, but decided he deserved a chance. She thought back to their conversation at the wedding. *Trust me, Emily. We will see each other again.* Kevin had gloated. But why did he want *this* job?

Unfortunately, her emotional struggle would have to be sacrificed for the good of the patients. She would learn to ignore Kevin, and his charming antics.

Silently edging her way past the board members,

Emily considered Kevin's possible motives. Whatever his reasons, one thing was for sure: when Kevin MacIntyre went after something, there was no stopping him....

She recalled the weeks he had spent trying to convince her to go on that first date with him. Flowers, phone calls, surprising her between classes. Yes, Kevin MacIntyre could write the book on charm.

Emily wondered how she'd face him each day, then rallied. *It's over now. We've both moved on. If he gets the job, well, if I can work with Bob, I can surely handle Kevin. I have to. The clinic's future depends on this renovation.*

Emily returned to her office. If the staff needed her, they wouldn't hesitate to call. She needed a minute to breathe. Time to collect herself and banish Kevin MacIntyre from her thoughts—if only temporarily.

Emily closed her office door behind her and leaned against it. *Dear God, help me. I don't think I can handle this alone—*

The phone rang, and she knew her moment of reprieve was over. She took two calls, then began seeing patients.

Twelve hours later, Emily pulled into her garage. She walked into the house, dropped her purse and collapsed on the sofa. Ignoring the blinking light on the answering machine, she set her pager on the end table and closed her eyes. She flipped her shoes onto the floor and propped her ankles on the arm of the couch.

It was days like this when she asked herself what she was thinking when she gave up the man she loved for that miraculous acceptance into medical school. And the answer was always the same. She had been thinking of her mother's struggle to provide for her and her sisters when their father walked out. She had been thinking of Katarina's hearing loss. Of the people she wanted to help. The last person she'd been thinking of was Kevin—the one person she should have considered more.

Her stomach growled, proclaiming that the salad she ate for lunch was long gone. She was famished. Dragging her fatigued body off the couch, Emily rummaged through the cupboard until she found a can of beef stew. The wind howled outside as a winter storm moved in from the west; snow was already sticking to the streets. *Thank goodness I'm not on call tonight,* she thought. Emily dumped the stew into the pan, turned on the burner, then simply stared at it, waiting for it to boil.

Kevin's words had haunted her for the past two weeks. *We can both be happy that you realized your career was more important than a family before it was too late.* They stung because after years of wondering, she finally knew why Kevin hadn't come after her. He felt she'd abandoned their dreams for a job. That truth was especially difficult after days like today. Days that started before seven and didn't end when the office closed. Days that melded, one into the other. Days when crises happened nonstop.

Help me to remember that it's not for my own glory, Father, but for Yours.

Emily couldn't accept credit for the many decisions that had led her through the last few years. For without Him, she couldn't have survived it at all. Medical school, internship, finding a clinic whose mission fit so perfectly with her own. It was nothing short of a miracle, finding her way back to Springville, Colorado. Or so she'd thought.

Until she saw Kevin MacIntyre standing in her patient's hospital room.

Until her past caught up with the present and threatened to crush her future.

Until Kevin made her realize she *couldn't* "have it all."

There were countless days when she wished for all the things that he'd accused her of rejecting for her career. Times when she longed for the serenity of a man's loving embrace. Nights when she dreamed of her own children. And still she battled daily with the green monster, envying women who had mastered that delicate balance between career and family. There were even moments when she cursed the day he had walked away. And days when she wondered if Kevin had ever felt the same.

Her eyes burned with tears she refused to shed.

It appeared she now had the answer. He'd moved on with his life. And on, and on, obviously not letting their broken promises slow his social life any. It appeared her mother was right. Kevin was like her father: a fifties type of man, who wanted his woman to raise the children and have dinner ready at six o'clock. Kevin MacIntyre was definitely *not* the man to offer support throughout her demanding career.

Snow swirled around the parking lot and drifted along the curb. Kevin closed the door of his shortbed pickup, ready to work out with Bryan at the gym before heading home. Cranky and ready to burn off some frustration, Kevin stepped through the glass doors and headed for the lockers.

"Hi, Kevin."

He turned, temporarily distracted by the silky voice.

"Evening, Kristen. Looks like life is treating you well."

"Could be better. You've been avoiding me." The brunette leaned her elbows on the handles of the stationary bicycle and flashed him an accusing smile. Perfectly shaped eyebrows arched high above blue eyes.

He returned the smile, inwardly calculating just when he'd last seen her, or anyone not related to the business. "No, it's not that," he stalled, suddenly tongue-tied and in a hurry to make an exit. "Work is keeping me busy. Maybe we can do something soon."

He ducked into the men's locker room, surprised when Bryan stepped in just behind him.

"Gone into hiding, have you?" his friend joked.

Kevin shrugged, wondering himself why he'd brushed the woman off. He and Kristen had dated a few times after she had decorated one of his model homes. Things had been going fine. Neither wanted a commitment. Both enjoyed the same things. So why did he find himself avoiding her as if she were trying to tie him down?

"How are Laura and the kids?" Kevin asked, hoping to change the subject.

It worked.

Bryan talked enthusiatically about his new family, and a few minutes later they headed for the weight room. Kevin was anxious to get back in shape before the longer days of the spring building season began. He'd put in more hours at his drafting table than actually working with the crew over the past winter, and it was beginning to show around his midsection.

"You okay?" Bryan eyed him accusingly some time later as he added another cast-iron disk to each end of Kevin's weight bar. "I've never seen you avoiding—"

"Fine, just bored with it all, I guess." Kevin lifted the barbell, only to be interrupted by another female acquaintance. After she left, Kevin sat up and wiped his hands on the towel draped around his neck.

Bryan elbowed him. "What were you saying about your life being boring?" His friend raised an eyebrow and chuckled.

"You're a newlywed. You shouldn't be noticing other women," Kevin grumbled.

Bryan snapped the towel in midair. "Don't worry, I'm perfectly happy where I'm at. Unlike you—"

"Let's get out of here. We aren't going to get anything accomplished in this place. Why don't we go get a bite to eat?"

"Thanks, anyway, I've already eaten."

"Oh." On the way to the locker room, Kevin suddenly realized that although he was busier than ever, his personal life had come to a screeching halt in the wake of his company's booming success. Now that he thought about it, he hadn't been on a date in months. What was wrong with him? No wonder he was irritable. *All work and no play...is bound to get on a man's nerves.*

Nothing was the same anymore. Dating had lost its appeal, second only to going home to an empty house and an answering machine full of jobs to pursue. Which was just what he had wanted—a successful business. He should be ecstatic. There were plans to evaluate, bids to make, orders to call in; business was right on track.

But something was still missing.

Bryan pulled his bag from the locker with a look of total satisfaction. To his credit, though, he didn't say a word. And there were plenty of choice comments he could have made. Kevin knew, because he'd used them all on Bryan little more than a year ago.

His friend got a drink from the fountain, then cleared his throat. "I still have that weight set I bought Laura at the house. Why don't we work out there?"

"I don't know if I'm in any mood to deal with disgustingly happy newlyweds and four energetic kids at this hour," Kevin muttered under his breath.

Bryan looked at his watch and laughed. "Another fifteen minutes and they'll all be in bed, anyway. Come on over. I need someone to push me before Laura's good cooking puts twenty pounds on me."

"You poor thing." Kevin considered going home, but quickly dispelled the unappealing idea. Unlike his friend, he had no one, nothing to greet him at home. No commitments. No leash. *Keep talking, Kevin. Maybe you'll convince yourself.*

"Come on. It'll be fine."

"Sure, why not." What was he bellyaching about? He had a business that was claiming more of his time each day. More than he'd ever dreamed possible. "I'll meet you back at Laura's—I mean, your house." He winced at the mistake. He still found it difficult to understand why his best friend had agreed to stay in the house his new wife had shared with her late husband.

"Don't let it bother you. I do it, too. It'll always be Laura's, no matter how many changes we make. She promises to start looking for our own house as soon as things settle down."

"With four kids, you don't plan on that being anytime soon, do you?" Kevin wrapped an arm around his friend's back and laughed. "Ah, wedded bliss."

Bryan elbowed him in the stomach. "I'll take the chaos of a house full of kids over a quiet one any day. You sure you don't have time to build a house for us this spring?"

"If I'd known you were going to be back in town and in the market, believe me, I wouldn't have filled all my slots. You wouldn't believe how many calls I've had this week alone. But if the bid for the clinic falls through, you'll be the first person I call."

"Not a chance. There's no way the committee can afford to turn you down. I'm glad to hear you're keeping busy." Bryan stopped beside his new four-wheel-drive and tossed his bag inside. "Let's get going. We can catch up while we work out. Laura will be glad to see you."

A few minutes later, Kevin stomped the snow from his shoes and followed Bryan into the turn-of-the-century home, half expecting an ambush.

The sound of happy children and the smell of fresh-baked cookies met him at the front door and tugged on his heart. Laura's youngest son, Chad, ran to Bryan and jumped into his arms. "Hi, Dad! Did you come home to tuck us in?"

"I sure did—wouldn't miss it for the world." Chad beamed at his stepfather's attention. "Have you brushed your teeth?"

The youngster scrunched his nose, then turned toward Kevin and said hello.

Bryan set his stepson down and patted him on the behind. "Get it done, and I'll be right up."

"T.J.! Kevin and Dad are here!"

"Chad, don't yell, please." Laura passed through the kitchen just as they did, and gave her husband a kiss. "You're home so soon? We've only been married a few weeks. You can't be that out of shape yet," she teased.

Bryan tilted his head toward Kevin and laughed. "Too many distractions there."

"And you came to this zoo instead?" Then, as realization hit her, she grinned mischievously. "Oh. You mean...*distractions*. Well, you may as well use that contraption you two brought me last year. It's going to rust if someone doesn't use it. I told you I didn't have time."

"I'm not giving up on you yet." T.J. ran into the room and gave Kevin a high-five, and Bryan let his embrace loosen. "Is Jacob asleep already?"

Laura playfully pushed him away. "'Already'? You haven't been chasing him since six this morning. I'm wiped out."

"Mom," their daughter beckoned.

"Just a few minutes, T.J. Kevin, please don't get him riled up, it's bedtime."

Kevin gave his friend's wife a salute. "Yes sir, lady."

Bryan kissed Laura again before she headed to the children's bedrooms, then turned to Kevin. "I'll help Laura tuck the kids in, and be right down."

Kevin and T.J. visited about school and sports for

a few minutes before Kevin sent the young man up to bed.

He could see why Bryan liked this chaos. He paused. *Don't go there, Kevin,* said an inner voice.

He and Bryan lifted weights for an hour, taking time to catch up on each other's lives and discuss business before he left. Bryan insisted he wanted to remain a silent partner because he knew nothing about the construction business, but Kevin appreciated his friend's willingness to brainstorm business tactics, anyhow. Just talking helped clear things in his own mind. And there was certainly enough to muddle his thoughts these days.

One of which was the Sonshine Medical Clinic bid. With Bryan's business sense, and Kevin's construction knowledge, they had come up with what they hoped was a winning proposal—one that would help the company remain secure for generations to come.

Laura sent a plate of peanut butter cookies home with him, another reminder of what was missing in his life. Homemade cookies...and someone to share them with. *A lot of good building a company is going to do—you don't even have anyone to pass it down to when you're gone.* He immediately thought of his father, and pushed the bittersweet memories away.

Kevin pulled the truck into the garage and climbed the steps to his empty house. Here it was, nearly ten o'clock, and he'd done everything possible to avoid coming home.

While dinner was heating in the microwave, Kevin showered and threw on a pair of ragged old sweats. Clearing that morning's breakfast dishes from the table, he poured a tall glass of milk and turned the big-screen television on to catch the end of the late news and eat his "dinner."

After the sports segment ended, Kevin switched off the TV, immediately deafened by the silence. He turned it on again and tossed the remote control onto the sofa, then retreated into his office. He clicked on the radio, hoping the noise would drown out the emptiness so he could concentrate on work.

He had already waited a week past the deadline to hear from the clinic regarding the renovations. If they wanted to break ground in a month, a decision had to be made soon. He couldn't afford to put off other projects much longer.

Having spent a year looking for the right project to launch a commercial branch, he couldn't believe it when he learned the best prospect would mean facing Emily on a daily basis. This decision came with a bucketful of mixed emotions. He'd almost backed away because of her; yet Bryan had convinced him to go through with it, even agreed to remain a silent partner to show his support and assure Kevin that he'd have the money necessary. They both knew Kevin couldn't manage the financial end without Bryan's investment. There was a lot riding on this bid. It was one thing to jeopardize his own financial security, but Bryan's and his employees' was another issue altogether.

The renovation of Sonshine Medical Clinic was a high-profile project with a strong emotional tie to the community. Even if Kevin lost money, if all went well, it would bring in more work than his growing company could manage. He wasn't going to get anywhere in this business by playing it safe. His dad's experience had proven that. In order to prove to himself and his family that he could have kept the family business going after his father's death, he had to do this, and succeed. Nothing was going to stand in his way. MacIntyre Construction would make it to the top, and stay there.

He looked at the note Bryan had given him and read the verse from the Book of Proverbs: "Commit to the Lord whatever you do, and your plans will succeed." Kevin shook his head, trying to maintain his optimism. If it's meant to be, it'll work out. *Think positively.*

Kevin perched himself on the edge of the chair, the clinic's blueprints spread across his drafting table. He took a deep breath and let it out, struggling to get his mind back on business. He looked at his changes. "Okay. We'll have to open this wall to do the extra wiring." He jotted notes to contact subcontractors as he went along. His eyes roamed down the sketch to the office with "Dr. Emily" in the corner. His mind drifted back to the day he went to visit Laura in the hospital and ran head-on into his past...

"If you'll excuse us, sir." Emily had said. No hello. Just that phony smile plastered across her face. Her disposition was as bristly as steel wool. Trying to ignore Emily, he had joked with Laura, leaving the poor patient in tears because it hurt to laugh after her abdominal surgery. Emily had mistaken Laura's tears for her feelings having been hurt, and the doctor had actually *scolded* him. So much for bedside manner.

Even angry, she'd attracted him. Affected him. Made him look at the years without her and see how empty life was. He faced the truth—he'd been living a superficial and indulgent existence. After nearly eight years apart, merely seeing Emily had changed his life—again.

Kevin slapped the ruler onto the paper and drew in the new wall. *It's strictly business, Emily. Strictly business.* He tried to erase the image of the unforgettable redhead from his mind. He didn't need to be reminded of the pain. Hers, or his. Eight years was a long time.

He had changed. The past was over. And love was out of the question—something to be avoided at all costs.

But handing my troubles to God just isn't as easy as it sounds.

Chapter Four

The phone rang, and Kevin let the answering machine do its job, glad the volume was turned down. He was in no mood to talk to anyone. The machine clicked off, and he returned to work. A couple of hours later he decided to call it a night. On the way through the kitchen, he pushed Play on the recorder, and was puzzled by the final message.

Kevin rewound the tape and played the last message again.

"How could you?" the woman's voice said.

"Emily?" He sat down at his desk and dialed the only listing in her name, but was intercepted by the clinic's answering service. She wasn't the doctor on call. He tried to explain the situation, only the receptionist wouldn't give out a home number.

He thought of calling Laura and Bryan to get her number, then realized it was far too late to call anyone. Besides, Laura would *never* give up her task as matchmaker if she knew he was trying to reach Emily.

That night Kevin slept fitfully, pondering what exactly she had meant by her message. *How could I what?* Could she have found out he was bidding on the job? No, that couldn't be the case. They couldn't reveal names on a silent bid. Unless they'd already hired another contractor. No, he couldn't even consider that.

If he didn't get the bid, he'd be furious she found out he had even been interested in the project. Knowing the way women think, she'd jump to the conclusion that he'd done it to be near her. Not a chance. It was business, pure and simple.

By dawn, he was just plain mad. He wondered why she thought she should have any say in his life at all. It was still too early to reach Emily at the office, and he had plenty to do before the clinic opened, anyway. After breakfast, he loaded his briefcase, tossed it into the cab of his truck and headed to the job site.

Kevin inspected the equipment, gave directions to get the workers going, then went into his pickup and pulled out his cellular phone. He called his office manager, relieved that she had a message for him to call the clinic director. Kevin called right away, encouraged when the director wanted to set up a meeting as soon as possible.

When Kevin asked to speak to Dr. Berthoff, though, he had no better luck getting hold of her than he had had the previous night. He considered leaving his mobile number, but decided against it. *Sounds like it won't be long before I'll have plenty of opportunity to talk to her.*

After getting the crew started on the two houses they were finishing, Kevin left for the clinic. Trying not to be overly confident, he gathered his courage and walked inside. He was escorted through the lobby, down dingy halls, and into the director's office.

"Kevin, I'm glad you called." The balding gentleman pumped Kevin's arm enthusiastically and motioned for him to sit down in the vinyl-upholstered armchair. Kevin could see why they were renovating. *Run-down* didn't begin to describe the place.

An hour later he walked out of the meeting with a new contract that would drastically change his life, one way or another. If all went as planned, he'd be doubling his staff size within the year. If not, he'd be jumping into the market looking for a new employer himself.

He turned left and headed to the lobby.

"Kevin?"

He'd know that voice anywhere.

Pivoting, he realized he must have taken a wrong turn and ended up near the examination rooms. Emily and another doctor stood shoulder to shoulder, having been reading a chart. He looked at the man, then to Emily, then back again.

"Excuse me, Bob. Unless you need this immediately, could we finish discussing it later?"

Kevin watched as the doctor assessed him. "Sure, why not over lunch?"

Emily's gaze met Kevin's as she gave the preppy doctor a curt response. "You know why not."

As if her punch needed help, Kevin mumbled sympathetically to Bob, "I wouldn't let it keep you up nights."

Emily paused momentarily to scold him with her eyes, then motioned for Kevin to follow her. There was a tilt to the corners of her lips, but he could say with certainty that it wasn't a welcoming look. "How are you, Kevin?"

"From the sounds of your message, maybe I'd better let you tell me. That was your *charming* voice on my answering machine, wasn't it?"

She walked into a cubicle with her name on the door, and he paused to examine the nameplate: Emily Berthoff, M.D.

Her answer was interrupted by the phone.

Taking the opportunity to collect information, he tapped on the wall, pretending to examine the structure. Her office was filled with books, books and more books. Same old Emily. Only difference was the titles. He could still picture her with her nose in those college textbooks. Heaven knows, he'd done his best to take her mind off her studies.... It hadn't worked then, and if he was smart, he wouldn't bother trying now.

The wallpaper here was outdated, even by his standards. There wasn't a plant, flower or photograph in sight. Nothing to indicate a family or a life beyond her career—

She ended the phone call and looked at him expectantly.

"I don't think I've had the chance to congratulate you, Doctor."

"Congratulate me?"

"On your degree." Kevin touched the rounded desk corner sticking out from under the stacks of books, files and journals.

"Oh." Her green eyes opened wide with surprise. "I never know whether to take you seriously or not."

Blast it, lady, don't look at me like that. I'm trying

to be nice. How could one sentence throw him all the way back to the day she'd walked out of his life?

Emily walked back to the door and closed it. "The last time we discussed my career choice, you were less than encouraging."

And now she was back, he thought. Every workday for the next six months. He had to keep peace between them.

"Whether or not I liked your decision is no longer an issue. I said 'congratulations,' and I meant it. It took a lot of work, and you deserve credit for it."

Obviously confused, she said merely, "Thank you." Emily put her hands in the pockets of her yellow blazer and took a deep breath. "Why, Kevin?"

Same Emily. Right to the point. "Why? I thought the message said, 'How could you?'" He smiled. "Don't I get some sort of congratulations for accomplishing *my* goals?"

"The way I remember it, your plan was to run your father's business. In fact, as I recall, that's why you stayed—and I left. Alone."

"Things changed. I have my own company now, which just happens to have landed a terrific deal." The elation inside was fading fast. He hadn't expected a red-carpet celebration, but even a half-hearted welcome would have been appreciated.

"So I figured out. Which was the meaning of my message last night. How *could* you bid on our project?" She stepped around the desk and looked him in the eye, as if trying to intimidate him. "Why this job? Why not some other building project?" she asked with more than a hint of disapproval.

"It was purely a business decision," he said,

meeting her challenging gaze. *Two can play this game, Doc.*

"A business decision?" Her voice caught.

"That's right, strictly business. Relax. It had nothing to do with you." He stuffed his hands in his pockets and jingled the change against his truck keys. He wasn't about to tell her how many times he had almost turned away *because* of her.

She ran her fingers through her hair, lifting it away from her face, and he felt his heart skip a beat. *Don't do this, buddy. She's off-limits. Business and pleasure don't mix. Remember that, whatever you do!*

"Surely there's another opportunity that would bring in a better profit than ours. As long as this is 'strictly business,' that is," she said tartly. Reaching for the desk, she closed a thick book and placed it on the jam-packed shelves. "How could you do this?"

Kevin crossed his arms and took a deep breath. "I could do it for the same reason you went across the country to your prestigious medical school. It was the best option available at the time."

She stared, a cold look that could build walls in an instant. Her phone rang, and she answered, still holding his gaze. "I'll be right there," she said into the receiver. Her eyes left his and she stepped around the desk. "I have an emergency."

He nodded, then opened the door and waited for her to go ahead. "Let's make a deal, Doc. I won't practice medicine, and you don't tell me how to run my business. Okay?"

Without responding, Emily rushed out of her office, and Kevin followed. Down the corridor, he saw a petite woman struggle to keep a stocky teenager, who'd obviously met up with someone's fist, on his feet. From the lobby, he heard the receptionist trying to get the woman to wait for a wheelchair.

"Here, let me get him." Kevin wrapped his arm behind the boy's back and followed Emily's directions. Once the patient was secure on an examination table, Emily put on gloves and began to clean his cuts. Kevin backed through the door, right into the doctor Emily had brushed off earlier. Through the opening, Kevin heard Emily tell the nurse to bring in novocaine and a suture kit, then turn to soothe the upset mother.

"Looks like Dr. Emily has it under control. Guess I'll go grab some lunch by myself," said the other doctor as he removed his stark-white lab coat and headed out the back door.

Kevin looked back at Emily, then walked down the long hall to the lobby. "If nothing else, this should be an interesting few months," Kevin muttered as he headed to his truck.

The remainder of the morning was a chaotic combination of reviewing applicants' resumes and ordering supplies. Always in the back of his mind was Emily, and the anger he'd seen in her expression when she saw him in the hallway.

But there was no room for second thoughts. He'd just landed the deal that could make or break his business. Emily had already met her goals, despite what they had cost her personally. He had let her go then, determined he wouldn't stand in her way.

Now, he'd be certain she didn't stand in his.

After getting his day back under control, Kevin called Bryan to tell him the news.

His friend bolstered his enthusiasm. "Told you they'd jump on your offer."

Kevin swallowed a lump of pent-up apprehension and felt a wave of relief, content that he'd done the right thing. "Yeah. They're having some publicity shindig Friday night to get the deal moving. As a partner in the business, you're obligated to attend, and bring your lovely wife."

"Sounds great." Bryan paused. "Hey, friend, don't forget, you're expected to bring a date, too."

A date. *Sure, why not. After all, this is a reason to celebrate.*

Emily zipped the crushed-velvet evening dress, then stepped into her black pumps just as the doorbell rang. "I can't believe I have to go to this reception for Kevin." She grumbled all the way to the front door. She tried to steel herself for a miserable night. Adding insult to injury, her car had had a flat tire when she'd left the office, and the first person to the rescue happened to be Bob Walker—Dr. Casanova.

She opened the door and met him on the porch. "Hi, Bob. I appreciate the lift."

"If I'd known a flat tire was all it would take to change your mind..." He smiled suggestively and lifted her hand to kiss it.

Emily pushed him away, amazed that a man with such a brilliant mind could be such a loser. "I don't want to go through this all evening. I won't. If I had *any* choice in the matter, I wouldn't even be going tonight."

"I wish you'd change your mind, Emily. All I ask for is a few minutes to explain."

"There's nothing to explain. I'm well aware of the facts of life. I think that was covered in basic premed, wasn't it? Maybe you missed that year."

"It was nothing," he began, following her to his car.

Emily opened her own door, ignoring his attempts to act like a gentleman. "One receptionist may have been nothing, the second one—"

"We never went out."

She dropped herself into a seat that barely cleared the ground. "Because she was married." Emily looked at him. "You just don't understand, do you, Bob? That is bordering on harassment."

"No harm in a little flirting." He shrugged, ignoring her warning.

She shook her head and closed her door to Bob's lame explanation. He'd blown any chances of a relationship with her, or any woman in their office. And now Emily was getting a headache, complete with a sudden case of the jitters. The last thing she needed was Bob next to her whining all evening.

Everyone in the clinic would be there to kick off the renovation. It was critical that she and Kevin be on their best behavior. Neither could take a chance of endangering their positions by revealing their past relationship.

Kevin's employees would be there, as would his silent partner and best friend, Bryan Beaumont. At least she would have Laura to visit with.

When they arrived, Emily walked into the restaurant as quickly as she could to avoid being paired up with Dr. Casanova. She was immediately greeted by Laura.

"Emily, I thought you'd never get here," Laura exclaimed. "Is this your new boyfriend?"

Emily turned around to see who Laura was referring to, praying it wasn't Bob. I can't believe I ever even considered dating him, she thought. "No, he's not. In fact, if Bob is any indicator of men these days, I'm through looking. Men just can't be trusted." She glanced at Laura, realizing she'd stuck her foot in her mouth already. "Oh, I know Bryan's different."

Laura smiled. "Yes, he is. But he isn't the only trustworthy man alive, you know."

There was a dreadfully long silence before Emily explained the situation with her car, ignoring Laura's comment altogether. She didn't need to expose her jaded opinions of men to a woman who'd found another wonderful husband after the death of her first husband. *Just because all the men in my life walk out when I need them most doesn't mean a thing, I'm sure. Who needs them, anyway?* "Would you and Bryan be able to give me a lift home?"

"I'm sure Bryan wouldn't mind. Let's go find him. Kevin was introducing him to some of your partners. I went to the ladies' room and haven't caught back up with him."

"Laura, I'd rather not..."

Laura touched Emily's arm sympathetically. "Kevin brought a date, so there's no reason to feel awkward. She's actually pretty nice."

A date? Why was she surprised? There was no reason Kevin shouldn't bring someone. In fact, she should be thrilled. What better way to avoid him?

They made their way through the crowd and to the hors d'oeuvres, finally finding Bryan at a table near the front of the room. Laura invited Emily to sit with her, which Emily was glad to do, until she realized Kevin and his date were seated at the same table. She glanced around, quickly realizing that most everyone had quit mingling—she had a choice between Bob's table, or Kevin's.

Friends had informed her that Kevin had started dating soon after their breakup. That knowledge was unsettling, especially now that she was sitting across from him and his gorgeous girlfriend. Laura was right: Kristen seemed amazingly likable. If nothing else, Emily would love watching Kevin squirm.

Emily sat down, and was soon listening as Kristen explained her work as an interior decorator, though her attention drifted to Kevin and Bryan joking together. Emily remembered with fondness their friendly banter. Ignoring the emotion building inside, she distracted herself from admiring how handsome Kevin looked in a suit and tie. The khaki blazer and baby-blue shirt accentuated the color of his eyes and complimented his curly golden hair.

She turned toward the raucous sound of laughter and the clinking of silverware against china across the room. Toasts were made to a successful project. Platters of shrimp scampi emerged from the kitchen. She and Kevin exchanged a glance. *Déjà vu.* Unexpectedly, the years between disappeared, and Emily found it impossible not to return Kevin's disarming smile.

Emily heard a pager beeping, and to her relief noticed Bob leaving the party.

Laura quickly jumped up and headed toward the ladies' room. Bryan quietly asked Emily to check on her, explaining that his wife had been battling the flu for a couple of weeks. Emily wanted to laugh, surprised at the naiveté of this father of four. Taking into consideration that his wife had left their marriage before telling him she was expecting, she simply patted his shoulder and followed Laura.

She went into the ladies' room, and wasn't surprised to find the newlywed blotting her face with a cold paper towel.

Laura looked up, a wan hint of embarrassment coloring her cheeks. "Are you here as a friend, or a doctor?" Laura took a mouthful of water, swished it through her mouth and spit it out.

"I'm not sure which you need more right now." Smiling, Emily stepped closer to the trim woman and felt her forehead. "No fever. Your husband seems to think you need a doctor. He hasn't a clue what's wrong, does he?"

Laura shook her head. She leaned her elbows on the edge of the sink. "He's had so much to adjust to. And contrary to what you think, we weren't trying yet. He wanted to wait a few more months," she mumbled through the soggy paper towel.

Emily let out a long sigh, struggling between her instincts as a doctor to agree with Bryan and the brief jealous longing of a woman. "Have you taken a test?"

"Who needs one? This is my fourth, Emily. The flu doesn't last two weeks. Besides, the office doesn't usually want to see a patient until they're ten weeks, right? I wanted to wait another week or two to tell Bryan. I don't want to worry him." Laura took a deep breath and exhaled.

"With your recent history, it wouldn't hurt to come in earlier, Laura—make sure everything's settled in the right place." Emily suggested Laura sit down in the soft chair in the corner for a few minutes before going back to the party.

Laura stood up straight and smoothed the front of her column dress, then brushed her hair back into order. She took a compact from her purse and applied some color to her pale cheeks. "That shrimp sounded so good, but when I smelled it..."

Emily could sympathize with a missed dinner.

"I wish I could see the look on Bryan's face when you tell him," she said to lighten the mood.

Laura's face paled again as she looked toward the creaking door behind Emily. "Looks like you may get your wish," she whispered.

Bryan peeked into the ladies' room and looked around uncomfortably. "Are you okay, honey?"

The concern in his eyes was obvious.

Laura closed the gap between them and hugged her husband, whispering in his ear. His face creased into a heartwarming smile. Bryan's hands were on her waist, and he pulled her closer.

Emily felt like an intruder watching the tender exchange of their kiss. Yet, much as she tried, she couldn't look away.

Bryan gave his wife one more hug, then held her at arm's distance and looked into her eyes. "Maybe I'd better take you home."

Emily interrupted. "I think that's an excellent idea. I hear jelly beans do wonders for morning sickness, which, by the way, can occur any time of day."

Laura glanced at Bryan, a guilty look on her face. "I should be fine now. This is Kevin's big night. You should be here for him."

Easing his way out of the ladies' room, Bryan shook his head. "You can't even stand the smell of the food, Laura. You know how protective Kevin is. He'd insist.''

''You can't tell him the news now. I don't want to overshadow his night.''

Bryan thought a moment, then turned to Emily. ''Could you explain for us, Em?''

''I'll tell him that Laura wasn't feeling well, and I insisted you take her home. He wouldn't dare argue.''

Laura broke into a wide smile, and exchanged a knowing glance with her husband.

''Don't get any ideas. Just doing my job.'' The two turned to leave, and Emily added, ''Bryan, I want to see her on Monday, just to be on the safe side.''

''Consider it done.''

The two left, and Emily felt tears sting her eyes. *This is ridiculous. You deal with pregnant women every day, Emily. Why should Laura be any different?*

Emily sat down and took a deep breath, willing herself to relax. Other women came and went, and each time Emily claimed she had something in her eye. Finally, she dried the tears, then splashed cool water on her face. She allowed her eyes a few minutes to clear before returning to the table to get her purse and leave.

But the elegant decorations—calla lilies and spires of fresh greenery—had been cleared from the tables, and the guests were already gone. She must have lost track of time.

Kevin and his date were making their way toward her. Kristen released Kevin's arm when he turned toward Emily. ''How is Laura?''

"She wasn't feeling well, so I insisted Bryan take her home." Emily looked toward the table for her purse. As if reading her mind, Kevin produced it. His hand looked incredibly tender holding the tiny evening bag, and Emily felt emotion choke her throat. "Thank you."

His gaze lingered, and Emily's heart raced despite the knowledge that Kevin's girlfriend had reclaimed her place beside him. "It seems your ride left already. Let us give you a lift home."

"No. Thank you, anyway." She glanced around, observing that the room was now filled with wait staff whisking dishes and linens into the back room. "I'll call a cab."

"It's bad PR to leave a member of the clinic board waiting for an unreliable cab service." He broke away from Kristen again, and pulled Emily aside. "Not to mention, I want to know what's really going on, and why you're upset."

She glared at him. "Now's not the time. You have a date." The last thing she needed tonight was to share her private misery with Kevin.

"I think that's up to me to decide." His eyes drilled intimately through her. "Let me get Kristen's coat."

"What?" She stared at him in amazement. "When did you become so cultured?" The words slipped from her mouth. So far, they had both been careful not to reveal their past relationship, and she hoped Kristen missed the inference.

"You might be surprised," he quipped, a teasing glint in his eyes.

When he returned, Kevin helped Kristen with her fake fur coat, then escorted them both to his truck.

The awkwardness didn't end when they all piled into the cab, with Kristen crowded into the middle.

Emily gave Kevin her address and asked if he needed directions. When he turned in the opposite direction, Emily glanced at Kristen. The woman's resentment was apparent. "Kevin, I need to get home," Emily insisted.

"I need to call it an early night myself. I'm sure Kristen understands, don't you?" Kevin's voice carried a tone that Emily knew all too well. The discussion was over. And from the look on his date's face, so was their relationship.

Kevin pulled to a stop in front of the woman's town house. Trapped between them, Kristen looked at Emily, as if it were obvious that she refused to exit the truck from Kevin's door as she had entered.

"I—I'm sorry, Kristen," Emily stammered as she got out to let Kristen exit. Kevin walked around the truck to escort his date to the door.

"I don't know what's going on between you two, but tell Kevin not to bother calling back until it's over for good this time."

Emily stared at the woman, who turned and began walking so fast on her spiked heels that her legs wobbled. Kevin trailed behind, and didn't seem surprised, moments later, to have the door slammed in his face.

Emily hurried to climb back into the truck before Kevin returned to help her. She hiked the hem of her dress an inch to step up onto the chrome running board, but her foot slipped. From the corner of her eye, she saw Kevin rush forward, too late to catch her before she hit the ground.

Chapter Five

"Emily!" Kevin dropped to his knees beside her. "Are you okay?"

She groaned softly, rubbing the back of her head. "I can't believe I did that."

"Well, it's a first for me, too. Never had a lady hurry just to avoid letting me help her get in. Guess that'll teach me to take two women home at the same time, huh?"

Emily lay awkwardly on the cold ground trying to explain how she'd fallen, but finally her irritation won. "Oh, forget it," she said, trying to get up gracefully. "Would you mind helping? Please."

He placed a hand on her shoulder to hold her still and leaned closer to examine her head. "You sure we should move you?"

"Who's the doctor here?" She squirmed, struggling to get to her feet. "I'm fine."

Kevin pulled her away from the truck door, trying to ignore the way her auburn hair tumbled from the curved silver clip and shimmered in the moonlight.

"Hang on." Kevin put one hand under her knees, the other behind her back, and lifted her off the ground. The touch of her hands on his neck brought back dangerous memories he would just as soon have kept locked away. He didn't move. He couldn't. His gaze dropped to her lips. All he could think of was the unthinkable.

"Kevin. Don't even..." she scolded, at the same time sending him a calculating gaze that half dared him to try.

He smiled, thinking about accepting the challenge, and his foolishness for even tempting fate. "Don't worry, Doc, I wouldn't dream of it." It didn't help when he saw the heart-shaped opening in the back of her otherwise conservative crushed-velvet dress.

She loosened her embrace, sudden panic in her eyes. "I think you should put me into the truck before your irate girlfriend finds us like this and gets the wrong impression—again."

He paused, then not-so-gently dropped her onto the seat and slammed the door closed. What was he thinking? He knew better than to play with fire.

They drove in silence for the first five minutes. "I've told you already, she's not a girlfriend. I mean, she was, but... She's not."

Her eyes glimmered with amusement. "You can say that again." Emily tugged the hem of her dress closer to her knees and began fishing around on the floor. "She certainly acted like she *thought* she was your girl, didn't she?"

I don't owe you any explanation. You can't even be civil! "What are you doing?" he asked instead to change the subject.

Emily continued to dig around on the floor. "Trying to find my evening bag and shoe."

"Your what? When did you lose those?" He pulled the truck to the curb and shifted into Park. Once the dome light was on, he joined the search.

"Sorry, but I wasn't thinking of my feet when you tossed me into the truck and slammed the door in my face."

Kevin muttered under his breath when he realized he had no choice but to turn around and go back to Kristen's. When they arrived, they saw both items laying in the driveway. Glancing at the glowing windows to see if Kristen was looking, Kevin jumped from the cab, retrieved the dainty black bag and high heel, then returned to Emily.

"What would Kristen think if she found these? She already believes there's something between us," Emily said with concern.

Kevin slipped the shoe onto her foot and set the purse in her lap, giving in to the temptation to flirt. He quirked his eyebrows and smiled. "I'd say she's a mind reader." Emily yanked her foot away from his hand and turned away.

"Let's get you home, before anything else goes wrong." He should have known better than to tease her—even after all these years. *The sooner I get you home the better.*

Emily clutched her door when he spun the truck around, making it lumber over the bumpy curb. "We'd have been fine if you had taken me home first. Everyone would have been happy. I wouldn't have a concussion, Kristen wouldn't be furious with you, and you…well, you wouldn't be stuck here yelling at me over something I had no control over."

"A concussion?"

She cleared her throat. "Okay, so I exaggerated."

Kevin let out a deep breath, silently assessing her fall. "First of all, if there's a chance you have a concussion, we should take you to the hospital and have you checked out." He drummed his fingers on the steering wheel, impatient for Emily to say something.

"I don't need to go to the hospital."

He wasn't about to leave her alone until he was sure she was okay. He'd had enough experience with injuries in college football to know the risks. It was too dark to tell much in the truck. It would have to wait until they got to her house.

"Second, I'm not concerned with how furious Kristen is. The only reason I called her is that Bryan insisted I should have a date." This was his fault. He should have called Emily a cab. Not that he cared one iota that this definitely ended any chances with Kristen.

He had known seeing Emily tonight would be rough, but he hadn't expected it to be this bad. It was a constant battle to remind himself that there was no longer any use trying to make the stubborn doctor swoon. It was obvious that she was convinced the breakup was his fault. Thinking back, he guessed it probably was as much his fault as it was hers, but would she see it that way? He doubted it.

In the long run, the family business was gone along with the original proprietor. His family hadn't been the same since.

She reminded him to turn south on Main Street. A few blocks later, he pulled into her driveway and ran around the truck to help her out. She stepped down, brushing him away. ''I'm fine. I can see myself in.''

''I'll leave just as soon as I'm sure you're okay, and not a minute earlier. Besides, you haven't told me about Laura yet.''

Emily winced as she put her weight on her foot. She couldn't let Kevin see her limping or she'd never get him to leave. And the last thing she could handle tonight was Kevin MacIntyre playing nurse.

''I couldn't help but notice that you showed up with Dr. Walker. Are you and he...you know.''

''If it's any of your business, no, we're not!'' Tempting as it was to make Kevin wonder, the thought of willingly allowing *anyone* to mistake her and Bob for a couple was out of the question. ''I had a flat tire when I came out of the office tonight, and he gave me a ride.'' She took a step, tentatively lifting the good foot. Her leg crumpled, and Kevin caught her. ''It'll be fine. I probably just twisted it a little.''

''Yeah, yeah, it'll be good as new in a few days.'' He offered an arm to lean on and helped her to the front door. She had no choice but to accept. ''Where are your keys?''

She opened the tiny bag, but realized she'd forgotten to move the keys from her carry-all in her rush to avoid letting Bob into the house. She let out a sigh of frustration. ''They're inside. I was in such a hurry, I forgot to move them to my evening bag.''

''Where's your extra key hidden?''

She closed her eyes and rubbed the lump on her head. ''I don't know. I don't think I have one.''

''Any windows open?'' he drilled impatiently.

She shook her head. ''Too cold out.''

Before she could argue, he swooped her into his arms again and headed back to the truck, mumbling under his breath.

"Put me down, Kevin. I'm not going anywhere with you."

"Are you going to play Casper the Ghost and go right through the door?" He stood by the truck and looked her in the eye. "You have three choices, Emily. I can leave you on the porch, I can call a locksmith, or you can come to my place for the night."

"I don't think so!"

He laughed cynically. "I thought you'd see it my way. Now listen here, lady. You have a lump on your head, a sprained ankle and a very cold porch."

"A sprained ankle? And what did you base your diagnosis on, Dr. MacIntyre?"

He paused, and a twinkle of moonlight caught in his eyes as his gaze met hers. "I've had seventeen of them. And amazingly enough, I limped just like you. As much as I'd love to stand here holding you, it isn't getting us anywhere. Open that truck door for me so you can sit inside, and we can take care of one problem at a time. I'll use the phone in the truck, since I assume you don't have your cell phone in that itty-bitty bag of yours."

Emily looked sheepishly at him and opened the door. Her mouth gaping open. It's over between us, isn't it? He abandoned me once, he'd do it again.

He watched her struggling for words. "Must be my charm, huh?" He laughed, but she couldn't. That was exactly what it was. She couldn't think with him holding her, helping her, taking care of her.

He set her down with care and closed the door lightly this time. She watched as he walked past the hood of his hunter-green truck, thinking *she* was the one who took care of people. No one took care of her. Even when they'd been engaged, he'd never taken care of her. *Maybe you never gave him the chance,* said a voice inside her.

Emily realized Kevin was talking, and turned her attention to the arrangements he was making for the locksmith to come to her address. He started the truck and turned on the heater.

"You warm enough?" Kevin switched on the dome light, then lifted his arm to the back of the seat and reached for her hair clip. "May I?"

An unwelcome chill went up her spine and she chastised herself. He only wanted to check her head. "I thought we agreed, you won't play doctor, and I won't play builder."

"Yeah, well, maybe next time, Doc. It's either me, or the hospital staff. Take your choice." Emily hesitantly turned her head so he could look for any swelling. He unfastened the clip and slipped his fingers through her hair.

She pressed her eyes closed, refusing to let herself think of the old days. He carefully touched the perimeter of the goose egg and let out a little whistle. "That's one nasty bump. Let's check your eyes."

She couldn't bear the thought of him looking into her eyes. It was simply too much. "I'm fine."

"Hmph," he said, handing her the clip. "It'll be a while 'til the locksmith can get here. Why don't you recline the seat while I dig an ice pack from my first-aid kit. I'll be right back."

She felt the truck bounce as he slammed the metal box behind the cab closed and climbed back in beside her. He broke the inner sack of the disposable ice bag and mixed the contents, then placed it behind her head.

Suddenly there was an uncomfortable silence between them. Their few attempts at a conversation went dry. A few minutes later, the locksmith pulled into the driveway behind them. After confirming ownership by checking Emily's identification, he opened the front door. Kevin paid the man and came back to the truck for Emily.

Once inside the house, he deposited her on the sofa and closed the front door.

"Thank you for the ride home, Kevin. I don't want to delay you any longer."

Ignoring her, he loosened his tie and turned away, pacing the room. "I know you don't want to believe me, but I'm really not the louse your mother made me out to be. Yet I'm not here tonight to start over, either."

She stared at his broad shoulders, at the curls of blond hair, at the tension in his jaw. Part of her wanted to cry at his admission, and another part wanted to laugh. Not as much had changed about Kevin as she'd originally thought. Cynicism might have overshadowed his sense of humor at times, but he was still as open as could be. "Thank you for clarifying that." She didn't know whether to be hurt or relieved. "However, you don't need to stay. I can take care of myself—been doing it all my life." She didn't mean to sound harsh, but the words had an unavoidable bite to them.

"I just want you to understand, there's no room for dreams of family in my life. We both have other things we have to do now. Life goes on."

"Why don't we just avoid seeing each other altogether?'' she snapped. How dare he presume she was even remotely interested in a relationship with him again?

''Come on, Emily. It may be over between us, but we can try at least to be civil, can't we?'' He straightened his back, and his eyes narrowed. ''Once I'm sure you're okay, I'll be out of here. But until then, sit back, relax, and tell me where I could find your coffeepot. We're going to need something to keep us awake.''

''Don't bother, Kevin. I'll be fine.''

Kevin glanced around the room, from the checkered sofa to the fresh flowers on the dining room table. Trying to close the door on his curiosity, he looked back to Emily, who was now falling asleep.

''Open your eyes, Emmy.''

They popped open.

''What day is it?'' he asked.

She looked at him, annoyed. ''Friday.''

''How old are you?''

She hesitated.

''Come on, Emily. It's not like we have any real secrets, is it?''

''Thirty-two,'' she admitted reluctantly, as if it would be news to him. He knew she'd be thirty-three in two months. Surely Emily didn't think he'd forgotten her birthday.

''Your sisters' names?''

''Lisa and Katarina. See, I passed the test.''

''Your boyfriend's name?''

She laughed. ''Nice try.''

He smiled. ''Never hurts to ask.'' He looked into her green eyes, noting there was no difference between the pupils. He continued to examine them, while stealing a peek at the woman inside—the woman he had known and loved long ago. There was an impenetrable wall there, and he felt a shock of disappointment zap him back to reality.

"You're free to go home. I know what to watch for—headache, nausea, dilated pupils."

"Time will tell, won't it?" He moved to a chair across the room. "Humor me, prove me wrong."

"It's been a very long day, Kevin, and I'd like to go to bed—er, get some sleep." She turned her body, dropped her feet from the sofa to the floor.

"You know I can't let you do that. Come on, Emmy, pretend eight years ago never happened, just for tonight. I'm not going anywhere." He slipped his loafers off and set them neatly next to the chair. After an uncomfortable silence, Kevin leaned back and crossed one ankle over the opposite knee. "So what's wrong with Laura?"

He saw a sad and pained expression flash in her eyes. "I think that's for them to say." She ran her fingers through her hair, allowing it to veil her face.

"Bryan said you'd explain. You have his blessing."

"She's my patient. You'll have to talk to them."

He'd never before seen her squirm like this.

"I'm going to go change. Feel free to leave." She stood, stumbling as she did so.

He stood up and took hold of her arm, steadying her, but she shook loose. "What's wrong, Emily?"

She hobbled down the hall and slammed the door behind her. Kevin felt his own stomach tighten. He checked his watch, confirming his suspicion that it was too late to call Bryan. Storming after her, he felt the panic rise inside. "Emily. What is wrong with Laura?"

On the other side of the door, he heard her crying. "Go home, Kevin. Just go!"

He turned the knob and stepped inside the room. "You okay?"

Her answer was clear as she blew her nose. Tears streamed from her eyes.

"Come on, Emily, you're scaring me. Is Laura sick?" Kevin took her by the shoulders and turned her toward him.

"She'll be fine."

"Tears and a diagnosis of 'fine' don't go together, Doc. So what's going on?"

Emily pulled away. The delicate straps that formed the heart-shaped cutout on her dress tightened as she hugged her arms to her body. Her long fingers wrapped around the black velvet, and she dropped her chin to her chest, exposing the delicate sprinkling of freckles between her shoulder blades.

He felt his strength waning and stepped behind her, tentatively placing his hands on her shoulders. "I'm sorry, Emily. Of course you can't break your professional confidence. I'm worried, is all. I don't want to see Bryan hurt again."

"It's not going to hurt him, Kevin. It's a joyous occasion."

He heard the slight hitch in her voice when she said "joyous," and realized what she was saying, or, more to the point, what she was feeling. What could he say without making things worse?

He wrapped his arms around her and pulled her close. She needed a friend, and, the way he figured it, so did he. So many times he'd tried to convince himself that he was doing the right thing in avoiding any serious relationship, but holding Emily like this, doubt reared its ugly head again.

He and Emily had dreamed of a large family at one time. Now that was gone. It had to be.

Kevin closed his eyes, wishing he, too, could shut out the pain. Watching his mother's health fail after his father's death, he had promised he'd never let anyone suffer the same way. And when his sister had lost her baby and home to a fire the next year, he knew he could never bear the pain of losing another love, and especially not a child. "Better to have loved and lost, than never to have loved at all" was a total fabrication.

He held Emily in silence, leading her back to the living room. He sure wasn't the person to comfort his ex-fiancée on this one. She didn't want or need to hear *his* prescription for avoiding love.

Where's a joke when I need it?

They sat in silence, Kevin holding Emily, realizing too late that he was brushing the hair off her face and that his lips were near hers. He gave her a chaste kiss, and backed away. "I'm sorry."

She didn't meet his gaze. "Don't be. Even a doctor needs a little TLC occasionally. Thanks. I really shouldn't keep you any longer."

He felt his chest pounding; his mind could only think of escaping unscathed. Or was it already too late?

Chapter Six

Kevin placed the tire jack under the bumper of the sporty teal coupe and pumped the handle. An hour later, he had the tire repaired and put back on the car. Kevin slid into the seat, turned the key and revved the engine. "Not too shabby, Emily," he whispered to himself, then returned to her house and knocked on the door.

He was asking for trouble. That realization had occurred around three in the morning, as he peeked in to make sure Emily was doing okay. Once the knot on her head was nearly gone, he could have gone home. But he didn't. Instead, he sprawled across the sofa and dozed off. Emily was still sleeping when he awoke and took the set of keys laying next to her purse on the table.

Just this once, he promised himself. He would prove that Emily's mother was wrong, that all men were not the same as Em's father.

Kevin would show her that they could put the past behind them without becoming involved. Show her that they could be friends. He'd do her a favor—just because. He'd hand her the keys, ask her for a ride back to get his truck, get on with his life, and let her get on with hers.

It was too late for them. More to the point, it was too late for him. The price of love was too high. Life was simpler without it. Love was for dreamers. And his dreams had faded long ago.

Emily opened the door, her pale face barely visible. "What do you want now?"

He stepped closer and pushed the door slightly with his foot. "Emily, you look awful."

"Aren't you charming this morning? What do you need, Kevin? I thought we agreed last night, our association will be strictly on a professional basis." Her voice had lost its strength—even angry, it sounded as weak as she looked.

"It will be, I promise. After you take me back to the clinic to get my truck."

"What's it doing there?" Her words slurred.

"I took your tire and had it repaired. Could you let me in?" He tried to stay calm. "I like your car," he added, trying to distract her while he eased his foot into the gap in the door. *It has spunk, just like you.*

Before she could answer, Emily collapsed, forcing his foot away and trapping him on the outside.

"Emily!" he yelled. He turned the handle and pushed, moving her just enough to get in, then stepped over her.

She was lying on the floor, a broken lamp next to her. He shoved the pieces aside and unplugged it before kneeling beside her.

"Wake up, Emily. Come on, sweetie, wake up for

me." He placed his fingers in the hollow of her neck to check for a pulse. It was beating strong. Brushing her cheek, Kevin felt a draft as she exhaled. It had been almost ten hours since her fall, and so far the only possible sign of a concussion was loss of balance, but that could just as easily be blamed on her sprained ankle.

"You're scaring me, Emmy. Wake up. Please." He mentally scrolled through the first-aid training he'd taken at the community college, then lifted Emily's bare feet above the level of her heart. A minute later she opened her eyes, blinking them wildly as she drew in a deep breath.

"What happened?"

Kevin put her feet on the floor, relieved that she was okay. "You fainted, I guess. Stay here, I'll be right back." He searched through the hall closet for a washcloth and soaked it with cold water, then returned. She remained still while he blotted her pale face with the cool cloth.

When she started to get up, Kevin helped her move to a chair. Her damp hair smelled like apples and tumbled over her sweatshirt. Kevin knelt next to the chair and leaned his elbow on one knee. "I'd feel a lot better if you would have one of your colleagues check you out, Doc."

She studied his face intently, as if she'd forgotten how angry she had been with him just a few minutes ago. Her eyes opened wide, and she leaned forward. "Are my pupils dilated?"

He blinked with surprise, then slowly smiled. "I thought we agreed, I don't practice medicine." Kevin rose to his feet, hoping that from a distance her full lips wouldn't look quite so tempting.

It didn't work.

"Just remember who broke the agreement first." A smile tugged at her mouth as she tipped her head for him to examine her eyes.

Forcing the temptation away, Kevin looked at her pupils, then shaded them from the light and quickly took his hand away. He was relieved to see them make the proper adjustment. "They look fine."

"I'm not nauseated," she mumbled, as if reviewing a medical file. "No headache. Eyes are okay." She shook her head slowly, rubbing her arm. "Probably just need to eat. I missed dinner, and maybe the shower was too hot. I should have cut it short, I guess."

"What does that have to do with it?"

"Dilates the blood vessels and sends the blood rushing from the brain. I heard the doorbell and rushed in here. Your diagnosis was right—I just fainted. It's no big deal."

He wasn't convinced. People didn't just keel over like that. Not without a reason. Must have been her fall.

Emily released the footrest on the recliner and leaned back. She ran her fingers through her hair, trying to make it look as if she was only fluffing it dry. The knot was gone. Her stomach growled. She had to get some breakfast.

"You okay?"

She looked admiringly at Kevin, then nodded. She had treated him horribly from the first time she saw him at the hospital, and yet he continued to be kind to her. "I'm just famished. Why don't I make us something to eat, then I can take you to get your truck."

"Why don't you rest while I make something."

Emily laughed. "I remember your cooking skills. I'll do it."

"Let me help, anyway." A mischievous glint in his eyes tempted her to put her anger aside.

Emily couldn't forget a time when she had really needed his support, and he'd let her down. *Forgive seventy time seven. You aren't asking much, are you God?* Who was to say anything would be different now? He'd come right out and told her he wasn't interested in starting over. Proclaimed that there was no room for dreams of a family. *What happened, Kevin? You loved children.* Then again, he had once loved her, too. And that had changed.

He stretched out his arm, offering a hand to pull her to her feet.

"So, think you could handle the toast?" She took his hand, accepting his help—again. His grip was firm, yet tender and reassuring.

The years of hard work were evident in the calluses and scars covering his hands. Their grasp lingered uncomfortably. She let go and headed for the kitchen, leaving the personal questions behind. She couldn't afford to let herself entertain old dreams. Not with this man.

Kevin made a pot of coffee and searched through the cupboard for dishes, while Emily dug through the freezer for a can of grape juice—his favorite, she realized as she set it on the counter.

She'd gone through enough because of him, and survived despite his dumping her. They'd both moved on. It would be okay. She was happy. She had a job she loved. A home she bought all on her own. What else could she want?

In silence, Emily pulled eggs and homemade wheat bread from the refrigerator. Kevin reached over the door and pulled out a bag of shredded cheese, bringing his face close to hers as she reached for the milk. ''Do you mind?'' His dimples betrayed him.

The faint remnants of his musky aftershave scrambled her thoughts. *Mind? Do I mind that you've found a way back into my life? That you're right here in my kitchen at eight o'clock on a Saturday morning? That you're* flirting *with me?* She snatched the cheese and tossed it onto the white ceramic-tile counter, next to the eggs. *You bet, I mind!* Emily avoided his gaze, not sure she'd survive one more glance into his baby-blue eyes. How dare he flirt with her!

Emily felt the scars of her broken heart being pulled and tugged by Kevin's familiar voice, his blue eyes, his very being. Her entire soul ached. She'd tucked and stuffed her feelings for him so deep that she thought they'd never resurface. Apparently she was wrong. Go away, Kevin. You're not supposed to have a place left in my heart!

She broke the eggs into a bowl and stirred them with a fork, while Kevin placed the silverware on the table and mixed the juice. Her gaze darted to him and back to the stove repeatedly, as if she were trying to convince herself that she wasn't hallucinating. Each glance served to remind her that Kevin was still very real.

When the eggs were done, she placed them in a serving bowl and headed for the table.

"Here, you forgot the cheese." He reached around her and tossed a handful of grated cheddar on top of the eggs, then paused.

Their eyes met, and Emily hoped he didn't sense the jolt of electricity that surged through her and made her shiver.

Kevin's brows furrowed, the sun-drenched skin around his eyes creasing with concern as he pulled away from her. "How are you feeling?"

"I'll be fine once I eat." They each carried an ivy-trimmed dish to the table and sat down. Instinctively, Emily bowed her head, noticing that Kevin had bypassed the grace and gone straight for his fork, then tried to retrace his steps without being noticed.

Emily said nothing, yet silently wondered about the changes she'd seen in only a few visits with the man she'd once loved. Who had he become in the time they'd been apart? *What happened, Kevin?*

Throughout breakfast, he kept her laughing instead of crying, visiting instead of arguing, and eating far more than usual. He watched, a glint of satisfaction in his eyes, as she devoured her meal.

Kevin had been her stability throughout college, watching out for her like an older brother before they started dating. He had always been willing to listen and had never shied away from her family. He had once helped her to take life less seriously, had cheered her up, had encouraged her. He had known how to make her smile.

He still did, she realized.

Emily felt betrayed by her own emotions. She was recalling too vividly the intimate sparkle in his eyes, the gentle way he'd taken care of her, his genuine concern for her happiness.

She looked at her watch. "I'm going to have to get going, Kevin. I have patients to see." It was as good an excuse as any to avoid prolonging this visit.

"I'll clear the dishes, while you finish getting ready." His smile was without malice, almost apologetic. For the love lost? For the years that could never be retrieved?

She longed for the courage to prove him wrong. To show him that his dreams hadn't died, after all. To show him that there was room in their lives for someone else.

Kevin realized he couldn't keep tempting himself, or teasing Emily, either. He'd given her plenty of opportunity to indicate the attraction was still there, and she'd backed away every time.

It was over between them. Just as she had forced her feelings for her father into oblivion, so had she allowed the love the two of them had once shared to fade with the passing years.

For a while, late last night, he had given in to the voice of his ego that said Emily was just being stubborn, that a little wooing would make the pain disappear. Then reality had intercepted and opened up the gaping wounds of the past. No, Emily needed a man who could give her all his attention, a house full of kids and a love that would survive the test of time.

True, there was a part of him that would always love Emily and cherish the time they had had together. But that was the past, and it was best left in the past. Today proved that. It was obvious she wanted nothing to do with him or the love they had once shared.

Later that morning, Kevin tried to ignore the memories of that feeling of togetherness as he walked into the empty trilevel house he loosely called "home." He'd never planned for a life of solitude. Never envisioned a life without love. Never expected life to turn out the way it had.

There was one thing that still mattered. He had his business back, and that would have to be enough.

Chapter Seven

Kevin juggled his work schedule to accommodate the new project. After hiring another crew and evaluating the clinic structure, he met with the electrician, the city's building inspector and a medical design consultant to make final changes on the renovation blueprints.

So far, Kevin had only seen Emily from a distance. Every time he drove into the parking lot and saw her sporty little car, he thought of the night spent taking care of her. He thought of how good it had felt to be with her, to hold her, to imagine the past was just a bad dream. But it wasn't. That night after the reception was the dream. A dream he didn't dare repeat.

He had a job to do, and nothing, and no one would come between him and its completion.

Kevin wiped the dust from his eyes, tired of fighting the spring wind. It was a miserable day to be removing windows, but he didn't have the luxury of changing the schedule. There would be enough unavoidable delays as it was, and there just wasn't that much extra time built into the contract.

As he moved in and out of the building, he could hear Emily laughing with the nurses, talking to patients and rearranging her schedule to help out the other staff. Kevin watched her leave at noon with the pastor who had performed Laura and Bryan's wedding. She returned looking carefree and happy, and Kevin was surprised to find himself wishing it were him bringing a smile to her face.

By midday, though, he could see the signs of stress. Was it her career, or his presence, or a really lousy day? he wondered. The smile she plastered on her face when their paths crossed was as forced as his own. He knew it, and no doubt so did Emily.

Don't get any ideas. She's a doctor now.

Kevin had lost faith in the medical profession when false hope had led his parents down a spiraling path in search of a miracle cure for his father's terminal illness. While his mom and dad had run from one doctor to another, across the continent and back, Kevin had attempted to run the family business. A year and a half later, when the residential construction market hit an all-time low, the business was all but gone, and so was his father.

Looking back, he realized there was no way a twenty-three-year-old son could have done anything differently. It was their money, their business, their decision.

Yet there were days when he felt that all he had achieved was to prolong his father's agony. While doctors had fed his parents' hopes, Kevin did the only thing he could to help—he kept the business operating. Despite Kevin's suggestions to revive the company, his older brother, Alex, convinced the family that it was safest to abandon the business in order to salvage a comfortable cushion for their mother to live on. With three younger siblings to worry about, Kevin swallowed his pride and closed the doors of MacIntyre and Sons, Incorporated.

Now it was just MacIntyre Construction. There would be no "Sons." Of that he was convinced. It had taken two years of back-breaking hours, working for someone else, before he'd been able to bankroll his own company. And finally, everything was falling into place, just as scheduled.

Right before calling it a day, Kevin called one of the new men over to help him nail plywood over the opening left from removing a window. Kevin sent Tom to the top of the scaffolding while he maneuvered the scrap into place. Both picked up their nail guns and began shooting nails into the wood.

Kevin felt a sharp pain in his upper arm and jumped back. The plywood broke loose and knocked him against the scaffolding. "What—!" He pushed the wood away, then turned his head, shocked to find a sixteen-penny nail protruding from his shoulder. "You shot me!"

"I what?" Tom jumped from the scaffolding, the commotion drawing attention from not only the crew, but the clinic business, as well. Kevin heard screams. A few minutes later, a nurse ran outside.

Kevin yanked the nail from his arm and immediately pressed his fingers on the injury. He looked down at the red stain on his flannel shirt. *I hate blood.*

The nurse rushed over to him. "You okay?" As she said it, she pulled his hand away from the injury, then pressed it back again. ''Let's go inside where we can clean that and take a better look.'' Kevin willingly followed, thankful he didn't have to do that himself.

As they walked inside, the nurse kept glancing at him. ''You feeling okay?''

''Fine.'' It was an exaggeration, but in a few minutes it would be true. He hoped.

''You're the boss, right? Kevin, isn't it?'' She had a look of interest that he'd seen way too many times in the years since his broken engagement.

He tried to be polite. ''Yeah, and you're...?''

She smiled eagerly. Too eagerly, he thought. *A year ago, I might have been interested, but not now.*

''Lois,'' she replied, motioning for him to go into the examination room to the right. ''You'll need to remove your shirt so I can clean that up.'' She turned her attention to the cabinet, pulling out a tray with a pile of gauze and some brownish liquid on it. He could almost smell the stench of iodine, and recalled memories of his mother cleaning his numerous cuts when he was a child.

He looked at the cut as he removed the shirt. *This is going to sting like crazy!*

The nurse examined his shoulder, and he looked away. He felt her dab at it with the damp gauze, tug on it, then dab some more. ''Hmm. When was your last tetanus shot?''

Kevin looked at the brunette, trying to remain calm. The one thing he hated more than blood was needles. ''Not too long ago,'' he assured her.

''Do you remember approximately what year? Maybe one year ago, five, ten?'' She dug through the drawer, seeming unhappy that the item she was looking for hadn't been restocked. She pulled an empty box from the cabinet and threw it away.

He mumbled a reply, not certain exactly which answer would satisfy her enquiring mind.

She laughed, and he realized he hadn't passed the test. "Don't waste your time, Lois. I don't need any shot. Just put a bandage over it, and I'll get out of your way."

"Let me get some supplies, and I'll have you back to work before you know it."

There was no problem, he assured himself when she left the room. She was getting a new box of bandages, was all. But the longer she took, the more nervous he became. *What's taking so long?*

Tentatively, he lifted the gauze from his shoulder and took a peek. All he needed was something to cover the cut. He stepped away from the table to look for a bandage himself. Not seeing any, he grabbed his shirt and headed for the door.

Dr. Emily intercepted him trying to escape. "Kevin? Where are you going?"

He lifted his eyebrows, almost pleased that she was no longer going out of her way to avoid him.

"Nice to see you, too, Doc, but maybe another time. I'm late to work."

"Not so fast. I understand you have a wound that may need..."

Kevin began to pull his shirt back on. The bleeding had almost stopped. "I'll just get a bandage from my own first-aid kit." There was no way he was going to let her near him with a needle.

She blocked Kevin's exit. "I need to see it, Kevin." Lois filed in behind the doctor with a plastic-covered tray containing several metal tools and bandages.

"Wait just a minute, here," Kevin stammered as he tried to step around the doctor, his hands in front of him as if to stop them both. "Emily... Wait, wait." He took a step backward and ran into the examination table.

"It's okay. It'll just take a minute. Let me look at it, Kevin." She stepped closer.

He moved to the side. "No, Emily."

He bumped into Lois, and jumped even higher.

Emily took hold of his arm. "Just let me look at it," she said calmly, a teasing look of satisfaction in her gaze. "We may not need anything except a tetanus shot." Her voice was authoritative yet soft, her touch strangely comforting, and her gaze—totally *un*businesslike.

If Tom hadn't made such a ruckus over a little mishap, I wouldn't be in this mess, Kevin thought.

Emily turned and reached for a bottle marked Saline Solution and a wad of gauze. "I'm going to irrigate it, make sure we get it good and clean," she explained.

Kevin recalled the tubes, needles and IVs that had failed to save his dad's life, and he began breathing more quickly. When Emily reached for his shoulder he ran out of the room and down the hall. He saw a back door marked Exit and bolted through it.

"Kevin!" Emily followed him through the exit, running right into a construction worker who was trying to complete the job Kevin and Tom had started. Had his employee not caught her, she would have landed in the mud.

Kevin turned in time to see Emily breaking free from the man's embrace.

He jumped onto a pile of plywood, stumbling as he leapt off, intending to hit the ground running. His shirt half on and half off, Kevin made a beeline to his truck. He'd get some ointment and a bandage, and fix his wound himself.

Catcalls followed Emily across the uneven ground, where an audience now gathered. Lois poked her head out the door, patients paused to watch, and even the crew watched with raised eyebrows as Kevin and his ex-fiancée danced circles around each other. Emily caught up to him as he pulled the first-aid kit from the back of the truck.

Kevin looked up, surprised by the firm warning in her green eyes. "This is ridiculous, Kevin. You can't even remember when you had your last tetanus shot!"

He held up his hands to stop her. "Thanks, anyway, Doc, I don't do needles. I'll just put a bandage on it." He winked. "I promise to take very good care of it."

His humor wasn't appreciated. Emily placed her hands on her hips, as if he were a defiant child. "You bullheaded fool. This isn't worthy of such a scene, Kevin. You can't take that kind of a risk." She took another step closer, and he backed away, stumbling over a clump of mud.

"Wanna bet?"

She let out a gasp of exasperation, then looked over her shoulder toward the people laughing and whispering behind her. "You're behaving like a child," she scolded through gritted teeth.

He forced himself not to smile. He loved the way

her eyes turned to a deep teal when she was mad. The dusting of freckles that bridged her nose seemed to glow like stars in the night sky. And her hair shimmered in the sunlight like a blazing fire.

"You can't afford to take a chance at getting lockjaw, Kevin. It can kill you."

He tried again and again to convince her that he didn't need any shot, but she remained firm, resorting to threats of making his crew help hold him down.

"You'd love that, wouldn't you? To make a fool out of me."

She smiled. "I don't need to—you're the one running away." She held up her fingers to show an inch. "It's a tiny needle. You'll hardly feel a thing."

"Famous last words." He hesitated, and the doctor made her closing argument.

"You could show a little faith in me, you know. Remember, I'm the doctor, you're the builder."

Kevin allowed his gaze to roam, noticed a frightened little boy watching. As much as he hated to admit it, he realized Emily was right. "Okay, I'll do it, but be gentle, would you?"

He followed Emily back into the clinic, watching her every step of the way. If things were different... But they weren't. There was no way he could be satisfied with a casual relationship with this woman. He had loved her too much, too deeply to make walking away a second time bearable.

Lois was waiting at the door.

"I'll take care of this, Lois, thanks." Emily stepped past the nurse, then waited in the hall while he went into the room and took his shirt off. Emily moved with confidence, trying to clean the wound gently, as Kevin studied the magazines, the lighting, the wallpaper peeling away from the corner—anything rather than looking at what she was doing.

"This might sting," she explained, holding up the bottle of brown liquid. "This should prevent an infection." She soaked a gauze pad and pressed it firmly over the wound, and he felt the liquid burn its way deep into the tissue of his arm.

As she opened the new box of bandage strips, Emily told him how to care for the wound, explained the indications of infection, and that he could expect a sore arm after receiving the tetanus shot. He suspected most of her spiel was to avoid the conversation turning personal.

A lot had changed about her, he realized. When they had first met, she'd been painfully shy, blushing when he took his T-shirt off to dive into the swimming pool. She'd been quiet and reserved, a sharp contrast to his own personality. He supposed that was what had first attracted him to her. She was a beautiful, intelligent woman with a giving heart. That much was the same. She was gorgeous, smart and still generous to a fault. But she'd also become stronger and more assertive. If possible, that made her even more attractive.

When he looked up, her gaze darted away as if she'd been caught admiring him. *Don't flatter yourself, Kevin. She's a doctor now. Seeing a man's chest is probably an hourly occurrence.* He wanted to laugh at the irony of his sitting here letting his ex-fiancée treat him. *Talk about playing with fire.*

She approached his opposite arm with the syringe, and her gaze strayed to his bare chest, then back to his face. Her cheeks turned a deeper shade of pink, and Kevin fought the satisfaction of realizing he *wasn't* just any other patient.

Despite trying to stop it, his smile turned to a chuckle. "Not much has changed after all, has it?" Before the words were out of his mouth, she stuck the needle into his biceps, and none too gently.

Kevin looked at his arm, felt a cold sweat spread across his chest and face. "Ouch. I thought you said it wouldn't hurt!"

Satisfaction twitched her mouth. "Consider yourself lucky it didn't have to go into the hip."

A laugh rumbled from deep in his chest. "You call that lucky?"

Emily's lips trembled with the need to smile, and she turned her back on him, then broke the needle off into the hazardous waste receptacle. "Have a lovely weekend, Mr. MacIntyre," she said, then walked out of the room.

Kevin was stunned. He hadn't expected her reaction, or his. Why did he continue to tease her? And why did she have to respond with such class? Why couldn't she just have slapped him and walked out? It was almost as if... No, it couldn't be.

He stretched into the sleeves of his shirt and buttoned it, then tucked the shirttail into his jeans before returning to work.

As soon as he stepped outside, Tom approached with an apology, followed by "Man, who in their right mind would run from a doctor like *her?*" The comment opened the gates to several bad jokes and offers among the crew to sacrifice themselves for a visit with "the doctor."

Kevin had been so focused on Emily, he'd not prepared himself for his crew's razzing. He couldn't react too strongly, or they'd be even harder to quiet. Not to mention that they'd realize the boss had his eyes on the doctor.

"What's your plan, boss? Playing hard to get?"

"Don't even go there, guys," Kevin finally said. When that didn't stop the crude jokes, Kevin called the entire crew together and explained that this wasn't a typical construction company. "A little good humor is one thing, but I don't allow trash on my sites." To his relief, the men respected his warning, and cleaned up their conversation.

Even so, Kevin thought he'd never hear the end of it from the crew. He was grateful when his watch hit six o'clock, and he could send the men home for two days. He hoped that when Monday came, the whole thing would be forgotten.

Emily had seen Kevin arrive each morning and had worked hard to avoid him; especially after looking out the window of her office one afternoon to see him hugging a blonde. The two had visited for a few minutes, then climbed into his pickup and left together. Memories of the breakup rushed back, which had actually made it easier for Emily to keep her emotions under control, until his accident yesterday…

When she heard Kevin was hurt, her attention went completely to him. She couldn't have thought of anyone else had her own life depended upon it. *What came over me? I can't believe I ran outside after him!* It went totally against her training, and she was ashamed of her lapse of professionalism. It had never happened to her before, and she'd be sure it didn't happen again.

Why now? she wondered. *Why, when I've survived our split, when I'm through the pressure of school, when I have a career that I love, does the only man who could ruin everything I've worked for have to return?*

How was she supposed to keep herself from falling in love again when he was right in the same building all day, and haunting her dreams all night? She tried to forget the way he had flirted with her in the examination room, held her when she cried over Laura's pregnancy, and comforted her with his tender embrace. She'd resisted him once, but knew she couldn't survive another dose of Kevin's charm. Her immunity just wasn't that strong.

She checked her watch and straightened the flowers she'd bought for the dining room table. Katarina was due to arrive anytime. The moving van had arrived the day before and had unloaded her sister's belongings into the garage, where they would sit until Kat could find a place of her own.

Emily started another load of laundry, then went to the basement to make sure the rooms were ready for her sister to move into. The second phone line for Kat's business had been installed earlier in the week, and the answering machine already had several messages waiting for the owner of Kat's Kreations.

Though it was to be a temporary arrangement, Emily had to admit she was in no hurry for her sister to find another place. She'd moved her own belongings upstairs with welcome anticipation. Having someone else in the house would be a wonderful distraction from her daily routine—wake, walk, work and wonder. She was tired of thinking about the past, the future and the man who wanted no part of either.

The doorbell rang, and Emily ran back up the stairs and through the house. She opened the door and lunged forward to hug Katarina.

She stopped just short of throwing herself at Kevin. She stumbled back. "K-Kevin."

"I'm glad to see you, too," he said, dimples again belying his stoic expression. Humor illuminated his bright blue eyes. "I'm awfully curious to know who that lucky person you *were* expecting is?"

She felt her cheeks flush and wished her hair was loose so it would hide her embarrassment. "Well, it wasn't you."

"That's a safe bet, now, isn't it?"

He glanced inside and lifted one eyebrow. "Am I intruding?"

She knew it was obvious that she was expecting a guest, and even if it was only her sister, she hoped Kevin would take the hint and leave before Katarina arrived and entertained any crazy notions of a reunion between Emily and Kevin.

"Well, if you're asking if I'm busy, the answer is yes. I am expecting someone."

"I need to talk to you."

"You couldn't call?" She licked her lips nervously. "I mean, I'm sure this is strictly business, right?"

He pushed his chin forward. "If I had your number, I would have called first. Unfortunately, it's unlisted, and you're not the doctor on call today."

"Oh." She glanced toward the street and invited him in, praying Katarina would be late for once in her life. "Is your arm okay?"

"Fine. Want to see?" He reached for the hem of his sleeve and pulled it above the wound.

She couldn't help but smile inside, relieved that he'd reached for the sleeve instead of removing the entire shirt, as she had momentarily feared he would. Noting the way his polo shirt hugged his broad shoulders, Emily took a deep breath. "It's a bit inflamed. Be sure to clean it with hydrogen peroxide and keep a small bandage over it to help keep germs out. You should also try some warm compresses."

"Nah, needs some air."

"If that swelling doesn't go down by Monday, you should come in and have someone look at it."

"Someone? Does that mean you're not going to be my doctor from now on?"

His doctor? She looked him in the eye. "I can't guarantee I'll be available," she answered honestly. There was a long silence. Then she backed into the kitchen and dug through the junk drawer for a piece of paper. She took a pen from the mug next to the phone and wrote down her number. "I'd prefer you page me, since my hours are so irregular."

He looked at the note then back at her, and tore the paper up, placing the tiny bits in her hand. "I don't want to talk to your pager any more than I want to talk to your receptionist, Doc. If you don't want to discuss this like two adults, fine. I'll handle it on my own." He turned and walked out the door, greeting her sister, who was on the way in.

"Will I see you again, Kevin?" Katarina asked cheerfully.

"Not likely, but have a nice visit, Kat" was the gruff reply.

Emily stepped outside, the force of his seething reply catching her off guard. Reality hit her like a sledgehammer between the eyes. If she had truly expected any less than directness from Kevin, she had underestimated him.

And if she continued to deny her feelings for him, she underestimated herself.

I still love him. The thought barely crossed her mind before another followed. *Please. No. I can't love him. He left me, just like my daddy.* She simply couldn't survive rejection again.

Katarina sighed. "Things aren't going so well, huh?"

Chapter Eight

Emily spent her weekend helping Katarina settle into the basement and introducing her sister to her new hometown. Together they perused the classifieds, looking for a suitable building to house Kat's Kreations, the growing mail-order craft business that Katarina had founded right out of college.

Emily assuaged her sister's curiosity with a simple explanation of Kevin's lack of desire for a family. Though it didn't truly explain anything, it quieted Kat's probing into a part of life Emily didn't want to discuss with anyone, especially her Pollyanna sister.

It was becoming more and more difficult to avoid running into Kevin at the clinic, yet she continued to try. She was not ready to deal with her unresolved feelings for the man. As it was, thoughts of him already intruded on her day. With each hit of the hammer, clang of metal and buzz of the saw, Emily wondered exactly what he was handling "on his own."

Monday evening, the outer door down the hall

clinked shut, and Emily closed her eyes. *Kevin is finally going home.* She let out a breath and set the journal aside, placing her reading glasses in the drawer.

"Evening, Doc."

She jumped, surprised to see the subject of her thoughts appear before her eyes.

When she didn't respond, he continued, stepping inside her office as he spoke. "I think it's time we get a few things out in the open, don't you?"

Kevin's jeans were white with dust from the plaster walls they'd knocked down that afternoon. Chunks of the same clung to his blond hair. He brushed his lips with the back of his hand as if trying to rid his mouth of the chalky residue.

The image was strong and manly, yet at the same time boyish and irresistible. It was no wonder Dr. Casanova was complaining that the nurses were more interested in the building project than their jobs. Having insider information from the females' perspective, she realized Bob was too proud to admit that his flirtations were now falling upon deaf ears.

"This can't go on, Kevin. I have a job to do, and you can't keep trying to distract me."

He chuckled. "Don't flatter yourself, Doc. If I was *trying* to distract you, you wouldn't stand a chance of resisting."

"Then if you're not trying to distract me, you wouldn't mind keeping your distance." She glared, feeling anger seething behind the smile plastered on her lips. She couldn't help but hear his cheerful greetings to patients echoing through the hall between her appointments. Not to mention the fact that the single female staff members were constantly praising "the boss" of the entire project as if he were the ultimate prize.

She knew better. Kevin MacIntyre was human, just like her, and everyone else. He'd made his share of mistakes. He had his dark side. His own faults and failures.

Kevin nodded. "And you wouldn't mind parking in the other lot."

"Excuse me?" She popped out of the chair and leaned forward, resting her hands on the cluttered desk.

"You heard me. You can park on the other side of the building. My work is on this side. I have no choice. I can't unload equipment from the other side." His stomach growled. The office had closed over an hour ago, and even Kevin's crew had abandoned the clinic before the sun set.

She watched his callused hand rub his midsection.

"Why don't we continue these negotiations over dinner."

She pushed aside the little voice inside that rattled off the list of questions she was too chicken to actually ask Kevin. Questions that would mean dealing with the past that, until seeing Kevin again, she'd quieted to a dull roar. Now they were blaring again. "There's nothing to negotiate."

He ignored her. "I need to eat. And I'm sure you do, too. You want to ride together?"

"No, I don't." Emily closed the file in front of her and set it in a stack to be returned to the records department, then reached for the next.

She felt his gaze follow her motions, yet he remained silent. From the corner of her eye, she could see him cross one leg over the other and lean against the door frame. *Not trying to distract me, my foot!* His tall lean body was a distraction all by itself, even coated with plaster. She resigned herself from pretending to work any longer and cocked her head as she looked at him.

"Why don't we meet at the café on the corner? Better yet, why don't we walk?"

Emily took her purse from the file drawer and turned back to the desk. "Because I'm going home. There's nothing else we have to say." Emily pushed up from her chair and grabbed her coat. Kevin backed into the hallway ahead of her, waiting as she locked the door behind her. She continued outside and turned toward her car, knowing the battle wasn't over yet.

Kevin took hold of her arm. "Please."

She paused.

He said "Please," she thought.

He didn't bulldoze his way into her office and order her to listen. He had said "Please." The tension in her jaw softened.

She and Kevin had plenty to settle. She couldn't avoid it forever. Maybe it *was* best to talk now, so she could move on with her life. She knew she wouldn't be able to forgive and forget him until they cleared the air.

"Fine. We'll get this over with." He smiled, his subtle way of letting her know he won without saying "I told you so." She glared at him. "Just say it, Kevin. I hate it when you gloat."

He wiped the smile from his face. "What?"

She walked past him, annoyed that he still made her heart beat faster. He hadn't even touched her, yet she felt her palms get clammy, her pulse rate rise and her temper flare. *How dare you come in here and make a mess of my life again, Kevin MacIntyre. How dare you walk out on me!*

Over sandwiches, they ruled out every idea they had to avoid one another. Halfway through apple pie, Emily realized the list was little more than a decoy—and worse, she was as guilty as Kevin for detaining them. She hadn't made one attempt to walk away.

Emily dropped her napkin on the table.

Kevin picked it up and reached for her mouth, wiping some food from her chin. "Neither one of us can afford any distractions from our work." His hand paused at her mouth, and he smiled. Slowly his fingers brushed her cheek, then he backed away. "We agree upon that much, right?"

She froze, momentarily captivated by his tender touch. *Don't back down, Emily. Just pick your battles.* "You asked me to park on the other side of the building. Fine, I'll do it. My office hours are between nine and noon, and one to five, so you'll have to arrange to stay on the other side during those hours."

"That's ridiculous, I can't do that. I'm the boss. I have to oversee the entire project." He looked at his watch and added, "Besides, it's well after seven, and you were still in your office. When do you want me to do my job, Doc?"

She didn't dare admit that she had only been here waiting for him to leave so she wouldn't have to see him. "Oh, yes, that reminds me—would you please ask your crew to refrain from their catcalls when I'm around. I don't appreciate the reminder of your accident."

He stared at her, and she wished the past eight

years could be erased. "And, would you please stop flirting in the office."

"Flirting? I haven't flirted with anyone at the clinic." His eyes opened wide, and there was an "I'm innocent" look on his face.

"And what about that blonde you were cuddling with the other day?"

He furrowed his brows. "Blonde?"

"Next to your truck."

"Elizabeth?"

She nodded. "Yes...Elizabeth." It dawned on her that Elizabeth was Kevin's younger sister. "Elizabeth? That was 'little' Elizabeth?"

He nodded. His voice lost its humorous tone. "This is ridiculous, Emily. Surely we can stand each other's company for six months."

"S-Six months?" she stammered. *No, Kevin, I can't do it.* She gathered her purse and slid out of the booth. "Just remember those boundaries, Kevin, and we'll be just fine."

"Emily..." He tried to get the waitress's attention, but finally tossed two bills on the table and ran out the door after Emily. She was at the edge of the parking lot already. He took off running, but by the time he got there, she was in the car and driving out of the driveway.

He stood in the middle of the lane, holding his hand up, forcing her to stop. Then he strolled to her window and motioned for her to roll it down.

"We've settled everything, Kevin. Just promise—no more distractions."

"You want to see a distraction, Emily?" Before she could answer, he leaned his head in the window and kissed her, slowly, just the way she remembered.

Then he leaned his elbows on the open window, the look of confidence replaced by astonishment. "No, I definitely don't think we've settled anything, Doc." He took a deep breath. "And I'm no happier about it than you are."

"Move out of my way, Kevin."

"We're adults, Emily. Let's handle it—now. You're accusing me of flirting, of interfering with your life. And up until that kiss, I haven't done one thing to *try* to distract you. I want to finish this discussion. Since your sister's visiting, why don't we go to my house, where we won't be interrupted? Looks like someone's come back to the office for something."

Emily took a deep breath and looked around, noticing a few cars left in the parking lot. True, the clinic parking lot was no place to be having this conversation. Especially after what had just happened. The last thing she needed was to have one of the other doctors see Kevin kissing her.

"Fine, I'll follow you there."

A few minutes later, Kevin pulled into the garage and met Emily at the front door. Walking inside felt like walking through a trap door. Her confidence faded, masked by confusion.

She couldn't believe he'd kissed her. With both hands on her hips, she confronted him. "What exactly was that about, Kevin?"

"Why don't you tell me, Emmy? You're the doctor—you analyze what's going on here."

Before she said anything, she tried to organize her confused emotions. He was daring her to admit the truth: that she still cared too much for him to leave the past behind them. "That was not strictly business."

A look of humor crept into his expression. "I'm sorry, Doc. I tried. I thought I could make it work. Then your lips asked me to kiss them, and..." His smile disappeared, and he looked at her tenderly, his gaze melting into hers. "I don't know what to do about it, Emily. I want to see you again, but the truth is, I can't offer you a future."

She paced the room like bait in a tiger's den.

How she hated the truth at this moment. Kevin could have lied and at least given her hope for a full recovery. He could have been the louse her mother predicted and abandoned her forever. But he didn't, and he wasn't. He was painfully honest, caring for her when he could just as easily have walked away. He was generous and giving, sensitive and...irresistible.

And how she hated him right now. How she hated his honesty.

Her lips tingled in remembrance of his touch, bringing back a flood of memories of a love that she'd thought would never die. Emily wrapped her fingers around her biceps, squeezing her arms until it hurt. These were questions she'd ignored for too long.

Her thoughts flew back to the day they had met in Laura Beaumont's hospital room, and she tried to keep the memory pure and unsullied. "Then what *do* you want?"

"I want you to forgive me. I want you to stop avoiding me. I want to figure out how to be friends again."

"Friends?" The memory of that kiss was far too

new for her to imagine a mere friendship between them. "Friends?" She heard the disbelief in her own voice, and was amazed when Kevin seemed not to have noticed.

Without any reservations, Kevin continued to talk. "You're obviously happy with your career, and I'm busier than ever with mine. It's obvious that neither of us has time for a relationship right now. And the last thing we need is our co-workers figuring out that we were an item at one time."

"An item? Don't you think it was a little more than that?"

He swallowed, and uncertainty crept into his expression. He walked over to the kitchen sink and poured himself a glass of water. "Engaged, then. We definitely don't need anyone to know that. The guys are already getting carried away with the nail gun incident. They don't need any fuel."

"Of course not," she muttered. The counter separated them. "We wouldn't want *that.* We wouldn't want them to find out you walked out on me when I needed your encouragement, would we?"

He was silent.

She turned her back on him and studied the living room, allowing herself the chance to learn more about the man Kevin had become. He obviously hadn't had Kristen do his decorating. His house was neatly organized, yet lacked a homey feel, and it was apparently the way he wanted to keep it.

She took a deep breath, determined not to let him see her pain. Emily felt it spread through her entire body. How could he kiss her, then tell her he only wanted to be friends? How dare he do this to her again!

Though caution told her not to, she had to ask. "I want to know what happened. Why you walked away. The truth."

She watched as Kevin resigned himself to her enquiry, leaning a hip against the counter. "I had to run the business, I told you that."

"You also told me it was a family business, that it was your responsibility, that it was our future. Now you have a different company in a totally different town. Since it wasn't just your dreams that were tossed aside, I feel I have a right to know what happened."

"My dad had cancer, Emily. Thanks to false hope from doctors, we were forced to shut down," he said bitterly.

Emily spun around to face him, torn between defending the medical profession, and comforting Kevin. "I'm so sorry, Kevin." He didn't respond. She stepped closer. "I won't try to defend what anyone told them, but I can tell you it's a very difficult job to give a patient who has less than a thirty-percent chance of survival enough hope to make him want to fight for life. I've seen what God can do when even medicine fails."

"Yeah, well, even that wasn't enough." He paused, then lowered his voice. "It's too bad our marriage didn't have those odds of survival, isn't it? I guess it was for the best. You have your career now, and I have no time for a commitment."

She stared at him, puzzled by the sudden irritability in his voice. "All this time, I thought—"

"What did you think, Emily?" Kevin looked at her with a sardonic expression that sent her temper soaring. "That I changed my mind? That I suddenly stopped loving you? What?"

"What was I supposed to believe, Kevin! You led me to believe it was because I wanted to be a doctor. How was I supposed to accept your parents' money when you resented me even wanting my own career."

"Don't throw that at me! We offered to help. You didn't want to be obligated to anyone. You didn't trust me, or them. And I can't even believe you actually thought I was chauvinistic enough to—" Kevin set his glass on the counter, then walked to the door and opened it for her. "You don't know me at all, then, do you?"

All the way home, she thought about Kevin's answer to her allegations.

It was all a blur. So long ago. How had she turned the MacIntyres' offer of help into Kevin being selfish and controlling? It seemed so different now. Suddenly, she was the one who felt selfish and controlling.

Was Kevin's father ill when they made the offer? Could she have helped change the outcome in any way?

Emily went directly to her room, too disturbed to even check in with her sister. From the depths of her closet, she pulled a flat box and stared. It had been years since she'd opened it. Each layer of tape represented a turning point in her recovery. The first, anger. The next, acknowledging the pain. The last, and she had hoped the final step—freedom.

It wasn't. Here it was again—this box of memories that she'd symbolically taped up and buried as deep in her closet as she had buried her feelings in her heart.

Dare she open it?

If she did, would she ever be able to close it again?

She kicked the box under her bed to get it out of sight. She wasn't sure she was ready to open herself up to any more pain. Emily showered, hoping that the routine would ease her tension and wash away the questions lurking in her conscience.

Kevin's kiss filled her memory. His anger broke her heart. She closed her eyes and let the tears wash down the drain, as far away as possible.

I'm not strong enough to resist him, God. And I'm not sure I could recover if he walked away one more time. Protect me, Father. Don't let me love him again if it isn't forever.

Emily dried off and put her pajamas on, then pulled back the heavy quilt and crawled into bed. The memories and random prayers continued. In the drowsy warmth of her bed, she felt at peace. Her anger disappeared. The feelings of helplessness subsided.

Chapter Nine

Emily pulled into the clinic parking lot later than usual, her mind still on the baby she'd delivered that morning. Since the employee entrance was now closed for renovation, she had to go right past Kevin to get to the main lobby.

As much as he visits, I'm surprised he gets any work done at all, she thought as she rushed past. Taking a slight pause from his conversation, Kevin added a casual hello. Still upset about his unexpected visit over the weekend, Emily muttered a greeting on her way past.

She'd found herself asking for more divine intervention since the beginning of the renovation. *Please help me to put the past behind me.*

It had taken years, but she had finally learned to let go of the pain from her father's abandonment. During college she'd come to accept that she couldn't be at peace if she was holding a grudge. It was the same with Kevin. Yet here she was again, struggling with emotions she had thought were long gone.

Inside the clinic, the last thing she'd expected was another delay, but Ricky West ran up to her and started telling her about the preschool's trip to a farm. Emily listened for a minute before hearing Kevin's voice again. "I'll see you in just a little while, Ricky. I have to go to work now."

Kevin's deep voice rounded the corner from the entrance to the lobby long before he did. "Here, let me help you with that."

A sweet voice thanked him, to which he replied eagerly, "Any time." Emily felt her emotions bristle.

Before having to face Kevin, Emily made a quick exit to her office. She tossed her jacket on the back of her chair and locked her purse in the desk drawer, then hurried to the nurses' station to get the file for her first patient. It was going to be a jam-packed morning. The sooner she busied herself with work, the sooner she would forget Kevin.

Three patients into her schedule, she entered the examination room to meet a new mother of six-month-old twins. She stepped inside and introduced herself.

The young mother's sweet voice echoed in her ears all day. It was a woman for whom Kevin had so willingly helped carry two infant seats in from the car. *I didn't think there was a man left who'd do that for a stranger,* she'd said.

Don't bother, Emily. No matter how much you try to turn him into your father, you won't succeed. The voice of guilt wouldn't give her a minute's rest. *Couldn't I have just one day without coming face-to-face with Kevin MacIntyre?*

When she left for lunch, she saw Lois and Kevin visiting outside, and turned away. For the remainder of the week, she forced herself to keep busy with work well past the time when Kevin was sure to have called it a day, which seemed to be later each evening.

Even that wasn't enough to free her from hearing all about him from the nurses. It seemed that his gregarious personality had all of the single women freeing their weekend schedules in hopes Kevin would ask them out. Come Monday, though, all were sorely disappointed. Everyone except Emily.

Despite her outward claim to not want to get involved with Kevin, she silently admitted that she'd be devastated if he asked any one of the nurses out. Inwardly, she knew it was all a last attempt to protect her heart.

In a matter of just a few weeks, progress on the clinic was beginning to show. The foundation for the new wing was poured and new walls were going up. Kevin's crew was working long hard hours, though not nearly as many as the boss. It soon became obvious that Kevin had the total support and respect of his men. In return for their efforts, rumor had it, he was quickly gaining a reputation in the industry as a fair and generous employer.

Emily caught herself looking out the tiny window in her office more than once, entranced with watching him work. It was a distraction she couldn't afford, emotionally or professionally.

"I'm sorry, Dr. Emily is with another patient." The pregnant receptionist straightened her back suddenly, then placed her hand on her stomach.

***I've never seen so many pregnant women in my** life as in this place!* Kevin drummed his fingertips on the gold-and-white-flecked counter. "When will she be available?"

The receptionist looked at the appointment book. "She's booked for two days. Do you need an appointment?"

He thought a minute. "She said to have my arm checked out if it looked worse, but she didn't mention needing an appointment. Maybe I can catch her before she leaves this afternoon."

"Just a minute, let me see if one of the nurses could do that for you without an appointment."

Before he could stop her, the woman waddled into the back room. She emerged a few minutes later with Lois following her. "Come on back, Kevin. It'll only take a minute to take a look at that."

That plan backfired. Okay, God, maybe next time You could let my timing work out better. How am I supposed to fix things with her if I can't get her to talk to me? Though he knew Emily was a busy woman, he couldn't help but be disappointed. In the past eight years, he'd dated plenty of women, not one of whom had left him with a burning desire to be a better man, the way Emily did. She'd had that effect on him in college, and even more now.

Over the last few weeks, Kevin had spent a fair amount of time in discussion with God about the irony of Emily's and his winding up in the same town. It was more than just a coincidence.

Shortly after Bryan's transfer back to Springville, his friend asked Kevin to join him at the pancake house every Tuesday morning before work for a men's Bible study.

There were issues he hadn't settled in his own mind, let alone with God.

The decision to join the group hadn't come easily. It meant becoming accountable to follow through with the changes he'd made in his personal commitment to God and to himself. Though he'd given up his footloose days, he still wasn't comfortable with the thought of attending church. Bryan didn't pressure him, though he asked Kevin to consider going with him, Laura and the kids, and to come over for Easter dinner afterward.

One on one, he and God were making progress. But he wasn't so sure he was ready to face the congregation.

He continued to struggle with turning his life around, giving up control, and, especially, putting his heart on the chopping block again.

It had been a long battle to recover from, letting Emily move on without him. With each family tragedy, resentment had taken a stronger hold within him. The years of rebellious behavior were over, yet the repercussions lingered as an ugly reminder of his weakness. Funny, he thought. Leaving Emily had sent his life into a tailspin, and finding her had set him straight again. Or, at least, given him the courage to get his life back in order.

Trouble was, it was easier to forgive others' transgressions than it was his own. If he couldn't forgive himself, how could he begin to hope for God's, or Emily's, forgiveness?

She deserved a husband who could share her dreams.

One who had dreams of his own.

He and Bryan met for their Friday morning coffee

before work. It had been a sleepless night for Kevin, and Bryan seemed to notice immediately.

"What's bothering you?"

Kevin grumbled and took a bite of eggs, chasing it down with a gulp of orange juice. "Nothing much, why?"

Bryan chuckled. "Nothing much, huh? Let's see. That either means work isn't going well, or your love life isn't going well."

Kevin gazed around, hoping no one had heard Bryan's smart remark. "Yeah, well, just shows how little you know."

"You and Emily had a chance to talk yet?" His friend took another drink of coffee.

"Yeah, we talk." *We just don't ever get anywhere with it.*

Bryan wove his fingers together and leaned his elbows on the edge of the table. "About?"

He looked up skeptically, wondering when his friend had taken over Laura's duties as The Great Matchmaker. "Mainly about how stupid it would be to try again."

Bryan lowered his voice. "You didn't tell her, did you? You'd prefer she think you just walked away rather than telling her life dealt you a lousy hand and you made a few mistakes."

"She still has her dreams, Bryan. It's best she keep them, because I can't give them to her anymore."

His best friend was still on his "honeymoon." He'd lost all objectivity. He believed love could conquer all, heal all, forgive all. Little did he know.

"Somehow I can't see Emily wanting or needing anyone to give them to her. But sharing them is another issue altogether, isn't it."

"She deserves better." He and Bryan had been through this countless times in the past few months. Watching Bryan and Laura overcome obstacles had given him hope, until he'd come face to face with Emily.

She wasn't any too thrilled to see him. He'd tested the waters, giving her a chance to knock down the walls between them, or at least leave the door open a crack. In their years apart, Emily had perfected the technique of batting down all passes—including his, and those by his crew. At least she wasn't discriminatory.

"I'm still curious why you think you're beyond forgiveness."

Kevin stared at the Ketchup-covered hash browns on the cast-iron platter. "I made a choice to disobey."

"And you think your mistakes are any different from the rest of ours? Don't we all make those choices, whether consciously or subconsciously? Is the degree of error in His eyes any different?"

Bryan looked at his watch, and Kevin realized it was time to get to the clinic. He placed a bill on the table, and both men stood.

"Open your eyes, friend. He's given you another chance to have everything you could ever want."

Kevin reflected on that for days before finally giving in to the logic. Even if He forgave him, Kevin reasoned, there was no guarantee that Emily could. Her scars went deep, and it would be like moving mountains to convince her that love could see them both through.

Chapter Ten

Kevin was reeling from the realization that Emily had spent the past years believing him a chauvinist. She had no idea how difficult it had been letting her go. How it had killed him knowing he couldn't give the woman he dearly loved her every dream. How far he'd gone to try to bury the pain of *her* silent message—that their love wasn't worth fighting for.

He watched the snow fall, remembering how much Emily loved winter. *I remember my dad making that pathetic snowman, I loved it. We had a snowball fight, and then he took us girls to a restaurant for hot chocolate.* The tears had blurred her vision and soaked his shirt. "Then what happened?" he'd asked. *A week later, Dad left, and never came back. We had so much fun together, and he left.* Kevin had held her and vowed never to hurt her.

Kevin shook his head. *I broke that promise. In her eyes, it was me that abandoned her.* "I'm sorry, Emmy. Honest, I am."

He drove to Emily's house, hoping she wouldn't kick him out.

Katarina answered, "Sorry, Kevin, she's at the hospital. One of her patients had an asthma attack. Care to come in and visit for a few minutes?"

Kevin turned and looked at the snow. He needed some advice, and Emily's younger sister could be just the right person to give it. "Sure. I have a few questions. Maybe you could give me some answers."

Katarina flashed her cheery smile, and Kevin let the encouragement soak in. He stomped his boots outside before walking on the beige carpet. Katarina closed the door behind him and took his coat, while Kevin untied his boots to leave them on the rug by the door.

"Would you like some cookies? Emily was up in the middle of the night baking them. Said something about a peace offering. You know what she's talking about?"

He followed Katarina from the entry to the kitchen to the dining room table. He eyed the flowers on the table and wondered who they were from. Seemed Emily always had fresh flowers. "Maybe."

"Maybe that's why you're here?" the perky blonde added as she poured him a tall glass of milk.

He pulled the chair out for her, then sat down across the oak table and moved the flowers to one side. "Could be, but I'll talk to your sister about that. How's your mom?"

The fine eyebrow tweaked high above Kat's blue eyes. "She's fine. Still works at the department store."

"And Lisa—what's she doing?"

"In her last semester of college, thanks to Emily.

Why do you ask?'' Katarina dipped the cinnamon-coated cookie in her glass of milk and took a huge bite.

There was no use lying. Kat would see right through it, anyhow. ''None of you have married yet, have you?''

The smile faded. ''And you think that's because of Mom?''

''I don't mean any disrespect, Kat, but it's quite a coincidence that three out of three are still single, don't you think?''

Kat was silent.

''She never liked me much, did she?'' Kevin took another bite of the chewy cookie.

''Mom has never approved of any of our beaus, Kevin. Don't take it personally. You want my opinion? She's incapable of loving any of the male population. She did not, however, pass along that trait to any of her three daughters.''

Kevin nodded. ''I suppose she had a few choice comments when Emily and I called off the wedding.''

Katarina laughed. ''Whatever happened between you and Em last night certainly stirred things up, didn't it? First, Emily can't sleep, then you show up with a hundred and one questions.'' She paused. ''Let's just say we've learned not to take our problems regarding men to our mother after that night.''

''Did Emily—go to her for advice?''

''That was a long time ago, Kevin. It's best just to pick up from where you are today, and move on if you want. Don't try to fix that.''

''You can't fix a problem if you don't acknowledge its existence.''

* * *

Ricky West was back in the hospital after a morning playing with a friend. The combination of ferrets and a sledding trip in a snowstorm's cold air had irritated his asthma.

She rubbed the stethoscope against her tunic to warm it up before pressing it against Ricky's bare back. There was still a loud rattle in the lower lobe of his left lung, yet his oxygen levels were rising, a sign that the nebulizer treatments were going well. His airways had opened back up, and Ricky was finally sleeping.

She turned to Ricky's parents. "I think he's through the worst of it now. It's going to take some time for him to get back to full speed."

"Thank you for coming, Dr. Emily. I hope we haven't ruined your weekend by calling you at home. I'm sure Dr. Walker is a very capable doctor, but he has no patience with Ricky."

Emily felt her heart swell from the compliment, but at the same time was hesitant to let herself care so much. "It's not a problem. That's why I gave you my number. I'll be back this afternoon to check on Ricky, I promise."

On her way home, Emily stopped at the grocery store, then drove to the church to pick up some supplies to prepare for Sunday school the next morning.

When she drove up to her house, she was startled to see Kevin's pickup in the driveway. She left the car in the drive, since Katarina's things were still occupying the garage.

She opened the front door, and was surprised to see Katarina and Kevin sitting at the table, eating cookies and drinking milk.

Kevin jumped to his feet. "Afternoon."

Emily wanted to believe his being here was a good sign, but didn't allow herself to hope for too much. They had been through ups and downs for weeks now. "Hello. I see you found my peace offering."

Kevin's smile took the chill of the spring storm out of her. "Best snickerdoodles I've had in eight years. I came to apologize for last night."

Emily looked at her sister, who had a grin that spread from ear to ear, then back to Kevin.

"Mostly, I'm sorry we didn't say more eight years ago, Emmy." He stepped closer and looked deep into her eyes. "We owe it to each other to talk it through, don't we?"

"What about demanding careers? And not dreaming anymore? And no commitments—"

"Are you saying you're not interested in going to dinner with me tonight?"

She glanced at Kat.

"Don't be a fool, Emily. We can go out anytime. Go on."

She turned back to Kevin and smiled. "I'm very interested. What time?"

"Now. Thought we could make a day of it, since we're both off. Speaking of which, do you always get called in on your weekends off?"

Shaking her head, she explained the situation with Ricky. "I need to check in on him again this afternoon. It won't take very long. I'm sure he's doing better now."

Humored over something, Kevin wrapped her in his arms. "That wouldn't happen to be the same Ricky that diagnosed you with a broken heart, would it?"

Emily felt her cheeks heat up. Leave it to Kevin

to remember that day with the precocious children at the preschool.

"I told you he was a very insightful young man, didn't I?"

He was gloating again. Only this time, she didn't mind. This time, she dared to hope it was merely the beginning of his gentle teasing in her life. There were still a thousand questions she had for him, but she would take them one at a time. For now, she would have to dream enough for both of them, to show him that the schedule of a doctor and the schedule of a contractor could be merged without moving heaven and earth.

She rested her hands on his shoulders, relishing the moment of contentment. "You don't mind my being a doctor?"

"Only when you try to come near me with a needle."

"You don't mind an independent woman?"

He grew uncommonly serious. "I never did. We really don't have to settle everything right now, do we? We have a birthday to celebrate."

Tears stung her eyes. "You remembered? Or did Katarina tell you?" Emily struggled, uncertain she should trust her own emotions. She wanted so badly to believe it would work out between them.

He looked for Katarina, who'd somehow slipped out of the room unnoticed. "I'm crushed. Don't you remember my birthday?"

"Well, of course, but it's rather difficult to forget a July fourth birthday, and the whole *country* celebrates your birthday!" Emily smiled, genuinely happy remembering the past. "What should I wear?"

There was laughter in his eyes, and his gaze softened when he looked her over. ''You're fine for our first event.''

Emily raised her eyebrows. ''First?''

''Put on your coat and gloves and follow me.'' He led her to the pickup and opened the door. A bulky package with a big blue bow sat in the passenger's seat. ''You'll need this.''

She removed her leather gloves and unwrapped the box. She pulled out a crumpled top hat, a ratty scarf, a carrot. *A carrot?* She looked back inside and pulled out two pieces of charcoal, and three large buttons. Confused, she turned to thank him. He was standing in the middle of her front yard with a large snowball in his hands.

''Happy birthday, Em. You going to stand there, or come help?''

''A snowman,'' she whispered. ''Kevin!''

''Better watch it, Doc, your tonsils are going to get cold with your mouth hanging open like that.'' He set the snowball on the ground and started packing more snow around it.

Emily tromped through the foot of freshly fallen snow and started a second snowball. ''Do you know how long it's been since I built a snowman?''

''Let me guess.'' He tipped his head as if doing so helped him calculate each year that had passed. ''Spring break, senior year of college, in Breckenridge, at precisely midnight.'' Kevin smiled. ''You take life too seriously, Em. And I'm here to remind you to lighten up.''

Emily's blush warmed her clear to her toes. She remembered the rest of that memorable night, and realized they would have a lot more issues to deal with than schedules and careers if this reunion lasted.

But not today. Like he'd said, they didn't need to answer everything all at once.

When they finished the snowman, it was nearly four o'clock, time for Emily to check on Ricky. "Why don't I go to the hospital and meet you back here in—" she looked at her watch "—say, an hour and a half."

"I'll see you then." Kevin stepped back and waved slightly, as if still uncomfortable with the sudden turn of their relationship. "Oh, and dress up. We're going to the theater in Denver."

Emily watched him drive away, then ran inside to shower and change. *I'll show you that we can work it out, Kevin.* Before leaving, she thanked her sister for understanding.

"If you—" Kat began.

"Don't worry, Kat," Emily said, holding one hand up to calm her little sister. She leaned closer. "I'm not letting him go this time."

When Emily reached the hospital, a nurse pulled her aside. "Dr. Berthoff, Dr. Walker had Maternity call for you. A patient is ready to deliver, and he's with a patient in ER. Seems there's been an onslaught of admissions this afternoon. Ten from your clinic alone. He asked you to handle the delivery."

Emily looked down at her dress and felt her heart sink. "Did you try to reach Dr. Gordon?"

"No one else is in town."

"Another hour, and I wouldn't have been, either. Would you tell Ricky West's parents that I'm checking on a pregnant mother and *will* be there to see Ricky as soon as I can. Then call Kevin MacIntyre and tell him I've had an emergency at the hospital and will have to call him when I'm through here. His number's in the phone book.''

The nurse turned and ran down the hall. Emily removed her heels and headed in the opposite direction. She put on scrubs, but since she hadn't even considered an emergency detaining her, had no other shoes to change into. She didn't trust herself on heels, and decided to put shoe covers over her stocking feet, but welcomed the sight of an old pair of tennis shoes offered by one of the nurses. Three hours later, Emily left the new baby in good hands at the nursery, checked in on the mother in recovery, and headed to Ricky's room.

Another hour of her date with Kevin was gone. ''What a start to a reunion! This emergency couldn't have happened a month from now.'' She reached inside her bag for the cellular phone to call Kevin. He wasn't home. Surely, he hadn't gone on over to her house. She called there, only to be greeted by the answering machine.

Her black leather coat slung over one arm, and her bag over the other, Emily exited the elevator and headed for the lobby. Due to the snow, she had chosen to park in the general parking lot tonight. She rounded the corner to the exit, and was surprised to find Kevin seated by the door, visiting across the lobby with the receptionists. ''Evening, Dr. Emily. This charming young man has been waiting for you.''

''Hello, Sally. How are you tonight?'' Emily's questioning gaze met with Kevin's smile.

''Rough night, huh?'' He rose to his feet, his suit wrinkled from an obviously long wait.

"Kevin? How long have you been here? I told you I'd call. You didn't have to meet me."

He took her coat from her arm and held it out for her. "I was worried about you driving through this deep snow in that sporty little coupe of yours. Besides, I thought you could use a smile." He extended his elbow for her to take as they walked through the snow.

She returned his smile, slipped her arm through his and told the receptionists good-night over her shoulder. A frigid gust of wind blew through the door as it opened. "I'm sorry about ruining your surprise tonight, Kevin."

"Doesn't look like Denver was a great plan tonight in any case. Don't you have boots?"

"I wasn't thinking of practicality, obviously. Would you like to come over to my house for some coffee?"

"Maybe after dinner. You haven't eaten, have you?"

She shook her head. "Where should we meet?"

"I'll drive."

She paused. *Here we go. Not even one date, and we're already disagreeing.* "My car is here, and I'll need my own car in case I'm called back to the hospital."

"You think I won't bring you back?"

She started to argue, but he interrupted her.

"Why don't I follow you to your house. We can leave it there. I'm still a little old-fashioned that way, Em. When I invite a lady to dinner, I pay, I drive and I walk her to the door afterward—even if it is slammed in my face when I get there." Slowly, his lips turned to a smile.

His humor was a refreshing change from that of the men she had dated throughout the years. "Had a few slammed in your face, have you?" She smiled back.

Wind swirled the snow around them, and he pulled her closer. "Enough, let's leave it at that."

"Hmm. I'll have to remember that technique. Is it effective?"

"Guess it depends on what message you want to send. There's only one lady who tried it and stayed a friend. Of course, that was a special circumstance."

Emily felt a twang of jealousy. "And who was that?"

He laughed. "Laura Bates. You should have seen the look on her face when I suggested we go skiing instead of what she expected to hear.

"Laura? You and Laura dated?"

As if he sensed her panic, he rushed into an explanation. "I wouldn't call it a date, exactly. I believe she called it an "outing." He told her about his canceled date, about wanting a chance to see how Laura really felt about Bryan. They'd gone to the theater, then skiing together, and through the course of his best friend and Laura dating, they had become special friends. To Emily, his concern for Laura's health now made a lot more sense.

They reached her car, and he brushed the snow off.

"I'll see you at my house."

"Be careful. There's ice under the snow." Kevin waited to make sure she wasn't stuck in the snow before going to his truck.

She smiled, enjoying being coddled by a gentleman for a change. She had to admit—Kevin knew how to treat a lady. Old-fashioned or not, she wouldn't argue any longer.

A few minutes later, Emily pulled into the driveway, admiring the snowman with his scarf flapping in the wind. Kevin pulled in behind her car and Kat's, then came around to help her get in. "Wouldn't you rather get some boots or even change into something warmer?"

"I'm not taking another chance at getting called in. Bob really owes me, now."

"He takes advantage of you, if you want my opinion," Kevin mumbled. She knew that but certainly didn't want to discuss it tonight, so ignored the comment.

Kevin helped her into the truck and went around to drive. A few minutes later he dropped her off at the door of the restaurant and drove around the building to find a parking place.

When they'd entered and were seated by the stone fireplace, Kevin ordered two cocoas and a platter of shrimp with cocktail sauce.

Emily felt a warm glow flow through her, and it had nothing to do with the fireplace. As much as she wanted to believe it was all going to work out this time, she was still inclined to guard herself. "Kevin, please don't make everything so perfect."

His gaze was soft as a caress. "We're a long way from perfect, Emmy. Just enjoy it for what it is, okay?"

"Which is?" She wasn't sure she wanted an explanation.

"Dinner with an old friend. Don't worry about tomorrow, okay? Let's take it one day at a time."

Easier said than done.

Chapter Eleven

Emily swung her arms in a quick rhythm opposite her feet; two more blocks, and she'd slow her pace. The spring sunshine had a crisp warmth, and invigorated her lungs. She hummed a melody in thanks for the beautiful day, and the fact that she had it off to enjoy.

It was Emily's first day to herself in a month. After the wonderful time she and Kevin had managed to find for each other over the past few weeks, she had hope there could really be a future for the two of them. There were no doubts in her mind that Kevin was still the man of her dreams. The man who would stand beside her, through good times and bad.

It was her mother whom she would have to convince—and Kevin. Though at this moment, she wasn't sure which would be more difficult.

Her mother had never forgiven her father for leaving her with three daughters to raise alone. She lived with bitterness to this day. Emily had grown up believing all men fit the same mold as Dad. Yet Kevin was the first man to show her differently. He would go for visits with Emily, ignore her mother's cold shoulder and smart remarks, and dry Emily's tears when they left. The day they broke the engagement was the worst day of her life—the day Kevin fulfilled her mother's lowest expectations.

Since then, though, there had been countless other "father figures" in her life who had helped her turn away from the fears and bitterness that had threatened to consume her, as it had her mother. God had given her the gift of freedom to move into other relationships with a sense of self-confidence and hope. Though she had sometimes slipped back, God had always been there to show her another happy couple who would raise her hopes again.

Then there was Kevin. Kevin, who refused to talk about the future, claiming he didn't want to ruin the fun they were having with anything that serious. His hesitation sent up warning flags, yet Emily was convinced that it would take only time for him to realize his dreams, as well as her own, were alive and waiting to be fulfilled.

She realized that changing Kevin's heart and healing his emotional scars weren't within her means. She could only accept Kevin into her life again, and leave the rest to Him.

After her morning walk, Emily dusted the table and placed the flowers in the middle. Once she vacuumed, she would have the day to relax, do some shopping and bake some cookies. The phone rang, and Emily answered eagerly, hoping it was Kevin.

"Emily!" Laura was sobbing. "Gretchen and Jack West were killed in a car accident last night."

Emily's voice caught in her throat. "Oh, no. And Ricky? Was he hurt?" She paced the room.

"No," she squeaked. "He was with us. They went to Denver for dinner and a play. They were going to be back around midnight—" her sobbing grew softer "—at three, I started calling their house, their cell phone, everyone I could think of. Finally, I called the state patrol and explained the situation. At six this morning, they returned my call with the news."

Emily thought of the precious little boy, and sank into the sofa. "Have you told him?"

"I couldn't. Bryan took the kids to the park to play, so I could start making phone calls."

Emily had first met the Wests during Gretchen's pregnancy, then at church. In addition to having them as patients, she had had Ricky in her Sunday school class for the past two years. As one of her first pregnant patients after moving to Springville, Gretchen had had a special place in her heart. It was Ricky who talked Emily into helping occasionally with preschool. "Is there anything I can do? Help find family, or..."

"I already have. I called Gretchen's parents." There was a long pause. "They can't even make it here for the funerals. I guess their health isn't good. Emily, could you go with me to Casper this weekend to take Ricky to see them? According to them, Jack has no living relatives."

Emily looked at her calendar. "Sure, I can fit that in. When do you want to leave?" They talked a while longer, and Emily agreed to join Bryan and Laura for lunch to tell Ricky about his parents.

As she completed her housecleaning, Emily's thoughts returned to Ricky. She wondered if he would be living with his grandparents for a while, or moving on to some other family member's home. She wrote a note to herself to make a copy of Ricky's medical records to hand deliver, thus bypassing all the red tape and the risk of their being lost in the shuffle.

When Kevin called after work that evening, Emily reminded him of the day at the preschool, and told him about the tragedy.

"I'm going to put a playhouse together at the preschool tomorrow. Would it help if I took him for a while?" Kevin offered.

For a man who doesn't want a family, you're awfully generous, Kevin. "Check with Laura. I'm sure she wouldn't mind at all. They're going to keep Ricky with them for the week."

"You want to come along?"

"I work 'til seven this week, so I'd better say no. But thanks for the invitation."

Laura and Ricky met Kevin at the door of the church and escorted him into the preschool, where the teacher was sitting in the middle of a pile of planks and pieces.

"Thank you for coming, Kevin. I'm sorry to bother you, with all the other work you have."

"No problem. Hi, Ricky!" Kevin squatted, resting his rump on his heels, to be close to the boy.

He listened as the little tike explained what had happened to his parents. Kevin gave him a hug, blinking back the unexpected tears in his own eyes. "It's really hard when your parents die, isn't it?"

Ricky nodded. Kevin jangled his tool belt and looked at Ricky. "Mrs. Beaumont called me to help her build something. What are you trying to make again?''

''It's a playhouse, but the instructions are missing. Laura can't figure it out. Neither can Bryan.''

Bryan's wife had already explained that her own husband passed the job along to ''the expert.'' Laura hadn't even tried any of the children's fathers, deciding she wanted the job done right the first time, before she left town.

Kevin studied the pieces and began experimenting. ''I think Ricky and I can figure this out, don't you, sport?''

Ricky nodded. He ran to the dress-up box and placed a toy hard hat on his head. ''Can I hammer some *real* nails?''

''Sounds like a great idea.''

''You're looking good, Laura. Feeling okay?'' he asked, glancing up. She turned pink, and Kevin laughed, thinking of how much Bryan loved making his wife blush.

''I'm feeling much better now that I'm into the second trimester.'' Laura sat on the pint-size school chair and reached for another plank to hand him. ''I hear Emily wouldn't tell you.''

''Who could argue with professional confidence?''

''Nice to know there is some left in the world, isn't it?''

He muttered a response, remembering how little respect he had had for it at the time. He'd been worried about Laura, and couldn't have cared less about ethics, he was ashamed to admit. ''When are you due?''

''Late September. Knowing my luck, it'll be October. My kids seem to have my sense of timing—

not a minute earlier than necessary. If you two are okay here, I thought I'd run and pick up some groceries while you work.''

Kevin looked at Ricky. ''Think we can handle it without Laura's help?''

''Yup,'' Ricky said, puffing his chest out.

Kevin put the frame together, then added the sides, encouraging Ricky to pound the heads of the nails until they were flush with the surface. An hour and a half later, just before dusk, they had completed the new playhouse. Across the street, three children were playing on a swing set, begging their preoccupied father to push them higher. The hopeful voices beckoned him, sending Kevin back to his own childhood memories—building a tree house, learning to ride a bike, wading in the icy cold stream learning the ''art'' of fishing.

''You're the only one standing in the way, you know.''

He turned toward the feminine voice, and Laura smiled. ''What?''

She was carrying a bench across the playground. ''I said, you're in the way, could you move, please? We want this inside for the children to sit on. You two did a beautiful job!''

''I helped!'' Ricky ran up to Laura.

Kevin jumped to his feet. ''You shouldn't be lifting that in your condition. Let me.''

He took the bench, realizing when he felt how light it actually was, that he was probably overreacting—to Laura, the children across the way, and to the guilt gnawing at his heart like termites in rotten lumber.

He had no business criticizing that father for ignoring his children, Kevin realized. He wouldn't even consider a family for the very same reason. He had no time. *Had none, or was he just unwilling to* make *time for a family?*

"I can't thank you enough, Kevin. The children are going to love this."

"We enjoyed doing it, didn't we, Ricky? If there's anything else, give me a call."

She helped him pick up his tools, and grinned mischievously. "Don't worry. I have your number."

Kevin thanked Ricky, then watched Laura help him climb into the Suburban.

Emily visited several times to see how Ricky was coping. As expected, he was angry and frightened. She knew from Laura that he was handling it the way any other child his age would. With Laura's past experience helping children cope with losing a parent, Emily knew Ricky was in expert hands.

One evening she decided to entertain the Beaumont children so Laura and Bryan could celebrate their six-month anniversary. Because of Laura's pregnancy, Emily wanted to lighten the emotional load Ricky added. She ordered pizza and gathered a few games for them to play. Kevin joined them eagerly, and Emily pushed aside the temptation to point out to Kevin his natural way with children.

She prayed each night that he would change his mind.

That he would want to make a commitment to her, and to a family.

That God would heal whatever had hurt him so badly.

Kevin pulled out the backgammon board and began setting up. Puzzled, Emily watched from the sofa, taking a break from reading a bedtime story to Ricky and Jacob, as Kevin began explaining the game to T.J. and Chad, the nine- and seven-year-olds.

After a while, T.J. became frustrated and stomped off. Kevin shook his head and followed T.J. up the stairs. A few minutes later they were back, sprawled across the living room floor playing the game again.

"Now, here's your home, and this area here is your yard, Chad." He paused. A few minutes later, she heard him reminding the boys that they always had to have a "buddy" with them or the other player could send them to the "time-out" chair.

Emily gave up trying to read. She listened, entranced by the way Kevin translated the game to the boys' level of understanding. By the end of the game, both boys were rolling the dice and making the moves on their own.

Jacob ran over to Kevin and dove onto his back. The two were especially close since Jacob and Bryan had shared Kevin's house. They rolled around on the floor, and Ricky watched quietly, staying close by Emily's side.

She held him close, wondering what he was thinking, remembering, needing. She was comforted by the fact that he would soon be going to his grandparents', where he would have plenty of time and attention.

As soon as she and Kevin had tucked the five children into bed, Kevin begged off duty to go over some bids that were waiting in his To Do pile.

By the end of the evening, she was exhausted and had an all new respect for Laura's gift of mothering.

"I don't know how you keep up with everything, Laura," she said to her friend.

Laura smiled, rubbing her round tummy. "It's one of those roles that you sort of 'grow' into."

Emily rolled her eyes. "Bad, very bad, Laura."

Kevin went with Emily to the memorial service, and together they spent the evening at the Beaumonts'.

"Dr. Emily, when will my mommy and daddy come back?"

Emily felt his pain, knowing what a blow it was to have a parent never return. Except Ricky's didn't have the choice her father had had. That wouldn't make sense to the four-year-old for years. "They can't come back, Ricky. When a person dies, his or her soul goes to live in heaven with God."

Emily looked to Kevin, hoping for some help. He remained silent.

"Why can't it come back here to live with me?"

"Why can't what come back here? Their souls?"

Ricky nodded.

Emily thought. "In a way, I guess they do. You have memories of your mom and dad that you can think about anytime. That way, part of them is always with you."

She asked him about aunts and uncles, to which he just shrugged. It was bad enough that he'd lost his parents, but it was too much to think of him having to move in with a family he didn't even know. Emily shared his confusion with Laura, who became silent. "What's going on, Laura?"

"He has no aunts and uncles. Just Gretchen's parents."

"The ones who are too ill to come here?"

Laura nodded.

Emily felt sick. She couldn't voice her concerns. They were unjust, and she knew it, but she just couldn't stop herself from worrying.

"His grandparents called yesterday and talked with Ricky. The bank called them to let them know there was a will. It's being sent to Casper."

Emily watched Ricky playing with Jacob, thankful that Laura and Bryan had been willing to open their home to Ricky temporarily. Not only was it good for him to be with a loving family, but it was especially comforting that he was familiar with all of them. Laura and his mother had been friends, and she was able to share memories of Ricky's parents with him. Since Laura's children had lost their father, Laura was already well-prepared for Ricky's endless list of questions.

Friday arrived, and Laura and Emily packed up the Beaumonts' Suburban with all of Ricky's belongings. The grandparents had already instructed the church volunteers to donate the majority of Gretchen's and Jack's belongings to the needy, saving only the things the women believed Ricky might be attached to.

Bryan and Kevin were there for support, and Kevin was the one who lifted Ricky into the back seat and buckled him into the car seat. "Take care, Sport."

Emily felt the tears well in her eyes, and was thankful that Ricky couldn't see.

Kevin closed the back door and stepped up to Emily. "You going to be okay?"

"I'll feel a lot better when I know he's in a good home."

Kevin nodded. "He's a tough kid. He'll be okay."

"Tough gets a person through a bad situation—not necessarily in the best mental state, though." Emily spat the correction automatically, then felt bad for criticizing Kevin's attempt to give her courage. "I'm sorry, I know you meant it as a positive attribute."

He smiled sympathetically. "Stay strong for him, okay? When you get home, I'll be here to be strong for you."

She wrapped her arms around his neck and kissed him. "Thank you."

"You're welcome."

The drive was long, and made longer by the barren winter landscape and dreary gray skies. Laura had packed several children's tapes and books to keep Ricky occupied. An hour after they left home, Ricky was sound asleep.

Emily looked back. "I don't know how Social Service workers do this all the time."

Laura chuckled. "Don't you find that comment a little ironic, Emily? You're a doctor. You perform surgery, bring babies into the world of couples who should never have conceived, and tell people they have terminal illnesses. And yet taking a child to his grandparents, you fall apart?"

Emily dabbed the tears from her eyes and added the tissue to the already heaping collection in the trash. "I can't explain it, either."

Laura reached a hand over to Emily's and squeezed.

They traded driving responsibilities halfway so

Laura could stretch out and rest. Laura had called home four times in the first two hours to remind Bryan of things he needed to do. Emily laughed at that.

"What's so funny?" Laura argued. "It's his first weekend as Mr. Mom."

"You don't think he'll remember to take his own son to the potty? Really, Laura. You're as pathetic as I am."

Both women smiled, a comfortable silence encompassing them. The mileage sign indicated they were almost there. Dusk was falling into night.

Ricky awoke, rubbing his eyes. "Look at the big boat."

Emily and Laura turned toward the bright lights in the distance, unable to tell exactly what they were looking at, yet unable to deny that it did look like a big boat. A gigantic ship, in fact. "In the middle of Wyoming?"

"Hmm. Remind me to ask George and Harriet about this. I'm sure they can explain what it is."

"Mommy and Daddy say it's a big boat," Ricky reassured them.

"A big boat it is, then." Emily smiled at Laura. They took the Center Street exit and turned toward town. Ricky's grandparents' house was settled in the older section, where charming homes had a character all their own. Ricky pointed to a house where a huge ramp had replaced the original stairs. "Gramma and Papa."

"Leave it to a child to lead the way."

"Are you sure this is it?" Emily queried, looking at the paper with the address, then searching the front of the house for numbers.

"I trust Ricky. Right, Sport?"

The toddler had unbuckled his straps and was looking for the handle of Laura's vehicle. Emily didn't argue, but watched in amazement as Ricky jumped down, hitting the ground running before Laura or Emily could stop him.

Whatever reservations Emily had immediately disappeared when she saw Ricky hug his grandparents. By the time they'd unloaded everything, Ricky was dragging his things to the upstairs bedroom.

Through dinner there was a sudden turn of the proverbial tables, when Harriet began drilling Emily about her life and beliefs.

After the meal was over, Harriet instructed George to take Ricky to his room to get ready for bed. Harriet was in a wheelchair, so George didn't argue. Harriet wheeled across the floor with ease, neither asking for nor expecting help.

The weekend went well, easing most of Emily's worries. While age and physical limitations were a slight concern, lack of love certainly was not a problem. Ricky didn't seem to mind that his papa couldn't keep up with him, or that he couldn't sit on his grandma's lap. There were young children living next door, and, according to Harriet, the mother was more than willing to allow Ricky to come over to play.

By seven o'clock Saturday evening, both grandparents looked exhausted. Ricky had missed his nap and fallen asleep on the floor in front of the television.

When Emily lifted the youngster to carry him upstairs, Harriet began to sob. Laura held the woman's hand in silence. Emily paused, then, at a nod from

Laura, continued. She dressed Ricky in his pajamas and tucked him into bed.

When she returned to the main level, the silence was ominous. "Emily, sit down, please," George asked. Once she had settled on the edge of a wing-back chair, George continued. "We can't thank you and Laura enough for taking care of our grandson this week, and for bringing him to visit us."

"This isn't a visit, George," Emily reminded softly. "You said he has no other family."

"He doesn't, but—" he cleared his throat "—Harriet and I aren't in any condition to care for a rambunctious little tike. We love him to pieces, but..."

Harriet finished her husband's sentence. "Our health wasn't an issue when they wrote their will, but Gretchen and Jack always spoke highly of you. We know they would want you to be Ricky's guardian."

Emily's mouth dropped open. She looked to Laura for support, and found a tearful smile on her friend's face. "B-But, you and George are his family."

"Oh, they had us as first choice, but knowing our age would one day be an issue, they wanted us to name a second choice in case we couldn't fulfill the obligation. The last time we talked, Gretchen suggested they ask you. I guess they never got around to it."

"Why me? I mean..." How could she tell them Gretchen and Jack weren't nearly close enough friends to have asked this of her?

"Gretchen trusted you above all others with her son, Emily. She praised your way with children, your professionalism, your..."

Emily looked to Laura. "You and Gretchen were closer than we were. This makes no sense."

"I also have four-plus children. I can't say with certainty that that had anything to do with their suggestion, but it would for me. Not to mention Ricky's asthma."

"That's another issue for us, Emily," George continued. "We don't have the knowledge, and I hate to admit it—but for Ricky's safety, I have to—I don't have the capability to keep up with his treatments."

"We would like for him to stay here to visit for a couple of weeks, if you don't mind. Mrs. Smith next door has agreed to help us for that long."

Emily listened numbly as Ricky's grandparents listed every one of her concerns. Their points were valid, but so were her own about becoming a parent. And they wanted Ricky to have a chance for a family with other children, something she couldn't offer him, she argued.

"Your odds are better than ours" was their reply.

Sounds like something Kevin would have said.

"Emily, Ricky has already lost his parents, and most likely we will be next. It's just not fair of us to put him through that again. If he has another young family, they will see him through."

She was a doctor with a sometimes demanding schedule. Kids needed time, had schedules of their own. How could she ever manage to fit more into her days?

Emily's mind reeled long into the night. *A child. Me—a mother. A single mother, just like my mom. What would I do when I had an emergency? I'd have to hire a nanny. I can't see me with a nanny in the house.*

And Kevin. This could send him running forever.

Kevin, or Ricky?

Please, God, don't make me choose between them.

Chapter Twelve

Emily had a difficult time telling Ricky goodbye, and found her own hesitation even more disturbing. The turn of events was overwhelming.

"You knew this before we left, didn't you, Laura."

"I didn't know for sure, but I suspected when they asked if I knew you, and if you could come along."

"You could have warned me it was coming." Emily shifted in her car seat. "I must have sounded like an idiot telling them why I shouldn't be his guardian."

"Knowing earlier wouldn't have diminished the shock, just made matters worse, I would think. You would have waited all weekend for them to bring it up. And what if I had been wrong? What if they had decided to continue to raise Ricky?"

"Guess it really doesn't matter any longer, I know now. What am I going to do?" It wasn't a question directed at Laura, and her friend seemed to understand. Silently, Emily went through the list of arguments at least a hundred more times in the four-hour drive home.

Emily had read the will, the wording of which did allow her to "find" Ricky a good home if she decided that was "best for all parties."

How can I know what's best, God? You didn't bring him to me as a baby. And why—when Kevin and I are just working things out between us? I love Kevin, Father. I want him in my life. Yet he doesn't want a family. I'm not even sure he wants a wife. How can I even consider bringing a child into the picture?

When she arrived home, a dozen roses were waiting on the table. Scrawled on an adorable teddy bear card was a note from Kevin: I'm just a call away, any time of day. Been thinking of you. Kevin. Katarina had left that morning on a marketing trip, so Emily had the house to herself for a few days.

She pressed her lips to the card and placed it back in the flowers. "Oh, Kevin, not today. I have too much to think about without letting you muddle my emotions more." Emily took her bag upstairs to her room.

In the silence, she tried to imagine the noise Ricky's boisterous personality would bring to the house. She considered how different it would be having someone else to take care of, to fix meals for, to get ready for bed at night. The exhaustion from spending that one evening with the Beaumont children was fresh on her mind. Though she would only have the one, she knew it would be a major adjustment, for both of them.

Emily emptied her bags and started the laundry, then baked a batch of snickerdoodles. She called Pastor Mike and asked him to see her early the next morning.

"Sure," Mike said. "I hoped you would call. Ricky's grandparents made a decision already?"

"You knew, too?" She could imagine Mike's wry smile on the other end of the connection. She and Mike had dated a few times, and had mutually decided their combined giving careers would be too draining on a relationship to make a marriage work, but the two had remained good friends.

"Yes, but I couldn't say anything. You know that."

"Professional confidence. I know," Emily mumbled. They were both intense personalities and took life very seriously. Emily valued him as a sounding board when she found herself too involved with a situation. "Well, the cat's out of the bag now, and I need to talk."

For a second night in a row, sleep eluded Emily. She was anxious to talk to Mike. The phone rang once, and she ignored it. She couldn't face Kevin yet. Tomorrow would be soon enough.

At six the next morning, Emily walked into the pancake house and ordered a hazelnut coffee while waiting for Pastor Mike.

"Morning. Penny for your thoughts."

She looked up, thankful Mike was finally here. "You may need to start charging for advice soon. This problem could bring in some big bucks."

Mike laughed. After several minutes of small talk, the waitress took their order. Mike looked at her with his deep brown eyes. "So what's the matter, Emily? Why do you hesitate to follow Gretchen and Jack's wishes?"

Emily picked up the coffee cup and began turning it around in her hand. The waitress approached and offered to refill it. "Oh, no, thank you, I don't drink coffee." She looked at it, puzzled that she *had* already drunk a cup. She must be more distraught than she'd realized. Emily set the cup back in the saucer and pushed it toward the waitress to take to the kitchen, then looked back at Mike, who was looking sympathetic and waiting patiently for an answer to his question.

"I'm a single doctor, Mike."

"That's not my fault," he said with a grin. "I tried to solve that 'problem.'"

She couldn't decide whether to laugh or cry. The indecision formulated itself as a lump in her throat, and Emily paused for a drink of water.

"Sorry, Emily, I'm teasing. It's just a wonder to me that you haven't found someone to share your life."

She cleared her throat. "That's part of the problem. I have, I think. Remember the man I told you about who wouldn't go with me to Maryland when I was accepted into Johns Hopkins?"

"The one who jilted you?"

The word sounded so much harsher now than it used to. She nodded. "He's back. We started seeing each other again."

He studied her, then added in his casual, jesting way, "Sounds easy enough. What's the problem?"

She shrugged. "Kevin says he doesn't want a family now—that our careers are too demanding. I know there must have been other things that happened after our breakup that hurt him, because he loves children. Kevin wanted a big family."

"And you care enough about him to let that stop you from taking Ricky?"

"I've never stopped loving Kevin."

Mike's expression changed; a smile spread across his face. "Kevin...Bryan Beaumont's best man?"

Emily blushed. "Yes. How did you...?"

Pastor Mike wiped his brow and smiled again. "He isn't the jealous type, is he?"

"Why—?" She followed Mike's gaze...right to Kevin. He was waiting to be seated, and simply tipped his head to her in acknowledgement. When the hostess came to seat him, he motioned toward the other side of the restaurant.

After her long, troubled night of soul-searching, the sight of Kevin made her fear all that much more real. "I can't tell him about Ricky. Not yet."

"You're going to have to sometime."

Emily moved to the edge of the booth. "Maybe Ricky's grandparents will decide they can raise him."

"Maybe, but I wouldn't count on it. They aren't saying they don't *want* him, but that they want what's best for him. And they've determined their daughter and son-in-law made a sound decision in naming you guardian, Emily—"

"Will you excuse me for a minute?"

Without waiting for Mike's answer, Emily walked up to Kevin and motioned toward the chair. "Do you mind?"

"I've only got a minute. I'm expecting Bryan and a couple more friends."

"I'm sorry I didn't call last night. It was a difficult weekend for me, and I needed time alone."

She could see the hurt on Kevin's face, even

through his smile. ''That's fine. We'll have to talk later—the guys are here.''

''Okay.'' Emily stood up and backed away. ''Morning, Bryan.''

His response was lost in the confusion of the others moving past to be seated.

When Emily returned to the booth, their meals had arrived, and Mike motioned for her to eat.

She couldn't. Seeing how she'd hurt Kevin made her lose her appetite.

Pastor Mike finished eating a bite, then looked at her. ''Emily, if I were in your shoes, I'd have the same questions, I'm sure. No decision is easy, especially when it involves the life of a child. You wouldn't be content with your decision if you didn't question it from all directions. That's who you are. That's probably the reason God led you into medicine. You don't stop with the easy answer.''

She cut her omelette and took a small bite, wondering if that was a compliment, or a concern in *this* case. Should she just accept Ricky without doubts? Was she wrong to find the answer such a struggle? She felt so selfish. What kind of woman would hesitate to take in an orphaned child?

That question alone had been enough to keep her awake all night. She'd tried to convince herself that there were thousands of people who would love to have a little boy like Ricky. That just because she wanted a child didn't mean *now* was the right time. That somehow, she would find just the right couple to take care of and give their love to the adorable boy.

Mike's authoritative voice recaptured her attention. ''As you make your decision, I'd like you to think about this story I heard: There was a woman who once asked God why she hadn't been blessed with a child of her own. And God said, 'You were. I did bring you a little boy who had no mother and no father. And I gave you a tender heart for him. He wasn't a baby, true enough, but he needed the care and knowledge and love that only you could give him.'"

Mike paused. "Emily, God's children don't approach Him in the same packaging." He swiped his head, then continued, "Some may be bald, and some may have beautiful red hair, and some may even have a past they would rather forget than deal with. Yet God welcomes each of us. It isn't an easy decision to become a parent, whether it be by adoption, or by birth. Having another person to be responsible for is a great gift, one worthy of much thought and consideration and prayer."

"Thank you, Mike."

"I'm sure you'll come up with the best decision for you and Ricky. And Kevin."

Monday morning had been crazy. Seemed everyone had been waiting through the weekend to call the doctor. She hadn't had a moment to think of anything aside from the stack of files she would still have on her desk at the end of the day.

She had just returned a patient's call and had been put on hold—

"Help! We have a man hurt."

Emily dropped the phone into the cradle and ran toward the construction area. "What happened?"

As she reached Kevin's crewman, he turned and led the way. The two rushed through the tarps and down the ramp as he explained. ''We were lifting the window from the truck, and it slipped from my hand. It knocked the boss to the ground. He's out cold.''

''The boss?'' Emily's heart stopped. ''Kevin?''

''Yeah, Kevin.''

Emily ran faster, nearly passing the man by. *Hang on, Kevin.* She turned to her nurse, who was trailing behind. ''Go get the COR cart.''

Kevin was motionless, laying on his back in the dried mud. Several men surrounded him; glass from the shattered window covered the ground. His skin was pale, and there were cuts all over his face.

Ignoring the glass, Emily dropped to the ground and knelt beside him. ''Kevin! Can you hear me?'' She placed her cheek over his mouth to feel for breathing, automatically pressing her fingers on his neck to check for a pulse.

''He's not breathing. There is a pulse. Call an ambulance!'' She wasn't going to take any chances, and there was no way she could chance moving him without a backboard. Emily saw one man holding a bloody rag to Kevin's head, and hoped he hadn't already moved the victim. ''Why's he not breathing?'' she shouted.

No one answered. Patti returned and dropped to her knees next to Kevin's head, setting the kit beside her. ''The ambulance should be on the way.'' Patti thrust his jaw forward, and Emily checked for an obstructed airway. ''Do you want the mask?''

Seeing nothing in his mouth, Emily tried to blow air into his lungs. ''Didn't go in. Try the jaw thrust again.'' Emily stayed in position, ready to move when Patti was ready. ''Don't you dare die on me!'' she said to Kevin.

Patti continued to hold Kevin's head steady and to pull his jaw farther forward. "You sure you don't want the Ambubag...?"

Ignoring her nurse, Emily blew two deep breaths into Kevin's mouth. "Nothing." She tore the shirt open and straddled his torso. "Oh, no, you don't, buster. You're not getting off this easy!" Weaving her fingers together, she straightened her arms and began abdominal thrusts, then moved back to check for an obstruction of the airway. Emily opened his mouth and looked, swept a red-and-white peppermint candy from his mouth, and resumed the position for rescue breathing.

"Got it! Let's start over."

Patti readjusted his jaw just before Emily's mouth covered his. Holding his nose closed, she gave him two deep breaths, and was relieved to see his chest rise this time. She checked his pulse. The beat was rapid. She checked his breathing, then breathed into his mouth again. "Come on, Kevin, you're not going to give up, are you?"

You wouldn't dare die on me! Don't you dare. She paused, then breathed for him again. *Please, God. Don't let him die. I need him.*

"Breathe, Kevin, three, four..." Emily continued the cycle as the ambulance's warbling siren grew louder, then came to a sudden halt. Kevin coughed—a weak but welcome sound.

Emily felt a surge of relief as voices ordered the crew to move back. A man at Kevin's head offered to take over.

Emily glanced up to the EMT. "He just started breathing again after I dislodged a piece of candy."

"We'll take over, miss."

"I'm a doctor, and I'm *not* leaving the patient. Get the backboard and cervical collars ready. A window fell on him. He could have spinal cord injuries. Possible concussion. He's still unconscious." One medic ran to the truck, while the other quickly wrote the vital information Emily was rattling off on a piece of white athletic tape stuck to his pant leg.

"Sorry, Doctor. How long did you say he went without breathing?"

"Two, maybe three minutes."

"But he's breathing on his own now? That's a relief." While he talked, he took a penlight from his pocket and checked Kevin's pupils. "Good job, Doctor. It looks like you got his airway opened fast enough. The pupils are still reactive. I agree, could still be a concussion. Too early to tell for sure, isn't it."

Knowing that Kevin hadn't been without oxygen long enough to cause permanent damage, Emily felt as if a huge weight had lifted from her.

The paramedic had gone on with his job without waiting for an answer. The EMT placed the oxygen mask over Kevin's nose and mouth. Then they slipped a *C*-collar beneath his neck and fastened it to stabilize his head. As they rolled him to one side, a large laceration was exposed on the back of his blond head. The other paramedic placed a four-by-four gauze bandage over the cut, while they slid the backboard under him.

"Cancel my appointments, Patti. I'm going with them."

Emily worked with the trauma unit until the ambulance reached the hospital. Once the emergency room staff began the exam, Emily emotionally stepped away from her role as a doctor and let the woman in love take over.

She backed into a far corner, out of the way, yet close enough to be assured he was okay. She couldn't leave him. She felt chilled and started shaking. She blinked back tears, watching as nurses prepared him for the myriad of tests to assess the damage.

Please, Father, don't let him leave me again.

Kevin dozed, a fuzzy image of Emily wandering around in his head. He rolled over, felt a tug on his arm, then remembered the IV leash in the back of his hand.

He flopped back and shook his head.

Don't you dare die on me!

Kevin groaned. *Must be the drugs.*

He heard Emily's voice. Felt her touch. "Emmy."

He'd seen a bright light, then immediately felt himself being pulled away from it.

Oh, no, you don't, buster.

Someone was squeezing his arm. "Let me go," he growled.

The feminine voice didn't go with the firm grip. "It's Darleen, your nurse. I'm just taking your blood pressure."

He blinked his eyes open, surprised to see a woman standing beside him. The room was dim, machines beeped, and something was pinching his finger.

"You feeling okay?" Darleen asked.

He closed his eyes again.

Don't you dare die on me!

He grumbled, then stretched his neck from side to

side. "I must have been dreaming. What happened? I'm okay, aren't I?"

"You're looking better every minute."

"Likewise." He opened his eyes again to see the brunette leaving the room. "Hey, you're not going to leave me all alone, are you?"

Darleen smiled. "You're not alone," she said, and continued out the door.

"You never stop, do you?" There was a welcome familiarity in that voice. He turned, greeted by Emily's smile. "Much as I hesitate to admit it, it's good to see you return to normal, even if you are flirting with someone else. How are you feeling?"

"I only flirt with *my doctor.* You should know that." He blinked sleepily. "What happened?"

She told him about the accident. "It was quite a head injury. I thought I'd lost you again."

"That why my head hurts?"

She nodded.

He lifted his hand awkwardly to his head, found the bandage and began to explore tentatively. "What's that?"

"Calm down, Kevin. You have a nasty gash with a lot of stitches. Don't touch, honey." She took his hand and lowered it to the bed. He wouldn't let it go.

She didn't, either. "You have a severe concussion, but you're going to be okay. We're going to keep you in here for a couple of days to make sure you're okay."

He closed his eyes and struggled to remember the accident, the ambulance, anything relating to the lost time. One memory he was certain of—Emily hadn't called when she returned from Wyoming. He was sure he'd seen her just before his accident, eating with some other man. It was breakfast. It was the last thing he remembered. He winced.

"Do you have any pain?"

Kevin squirmed, sweaty and itchy from the plastic-covered mattress and pillow. "Yeah, there's this one pain."

"Where?"

"I'd better not say, you'd accuse me of flirting."

She scowled at him. "I'm serious."

"You always have been. No reason for that to change now, is there?" He squeezed her hand tighter.

"Well, your memory seems to be good." She took hold of his other hand and spread both arms wide. "Squeeze both of my fingers."

He did as she told him, gazing into her eyes as she studied his coordination. She was beautiful. *Thank You for letting me come back to her, God.*

"Okay, that's good. You can let go now."

He shook his head. "Nope." He pulled her close.

"Nope?" He saw the teasing in her gaze, followed by a sudden look of concern. "Kevin, your doctor could walk in at any time."

"*My* doctor *is* here. Whatever happened to bedside manners, Doc?"

She blushed. "If you don't behave, I'll turn you over to a doctor with *no* bedside manner."

"You mean there are two of you?" He smiled. "Come on, Emmy, one little kiss."

"You're incorrigible." Her eyes drifted closed and her lips touched his. It was a slow, drugging kiss that left him feeling weak. He felt his body relax against the bed as she backed away.

His eyes remained closed, and he was transported

to his own dreamy world. "That was you." He furrowed his brow and opened his eyes.

Her look of anticipation offered hope. "When?"

"I don't know for sure. While I was out, maybe? Wait a minute. You were the one to save my life? You were talking to me. It was you...."

Her voicc was soft. "I wasn't talking, buster, I was yelling." A tear trickled down her cheek as she hesitantly leaned forward and kissed him once more. "Don't you *dare* do that to me again."

The depth of her emotion confused him. Things were getting serious, and he wasn't sure that was a good idea. Kevin studied her for a minute before coming up with a light response. "Oh, then I suppose you don't want me to mention that you were all over me. Or those loving comments you made. Very unprofessional, if I might say. You might think I didn't hear you, but I did," he teased.

She arched an eyebrow, and stepped close to the bed, her cheeks regaining a subtle glow that softened the worry lines on her face. "I guess you have the wrong person, after all."

Kevin laughed. "Oh, no, it was definitely you. And there was this bald guy." Kevin tried to remember who that was. He gathered by Emily's affections tonight that his first assumption was way off base. Maybe the bald man was his other doctor.

Her green eyes were brilliant and twinkled as if she had a wonderful secret to tell. Red curls tumbled over her shoulders. "You remember the pastor's visit?"

"The pastor?" He thought, suddenly apprehensive. There was something more he felt he should know about the man. *Why can't I remember anything?* "No."

She was disappointed. He could see it in her eyes. Why did she care that he couldn't remember a visit from the pastor?

"Hmm. Your other doctor will be in shortly to examine you. You know, the one with *no* bedside manner." Emily strolled to the door, then hesitated. "I'd better go check on my own patients before it's too late. I'll be back to see you first thing in the morning."

"Sweet dreams, Doc."

Chapter Thirteen

Emily called the hospital in the middle of the night, hoping to ease her concerns that Kevin's condition hadn't worsened.

Get some rest, she told herself.

It was impossible.

"I'll never tell anyone *that* again!" she said aloud.

Each time she thought of Kevin's accident, she felt guilty for not calling him after returning from Wyoming. Had he been angry with her instead of concentrating on his work? Was she at least partially to blame for what had happened?

After a sleepless night evaluating every aspect of Kevin's injuries and what his recovery would mean to his work, Emily began to worry. How solvent was his company? Had he overextended himself? Would he lose his business if he missed the deadline?

Kevin needed time off, and he wasn't the type to sit back and let others do his work.

She pondered the problem. Kevin and his crew

started around seven. Would his crew be able to continue working without Kevin at the helm?

On her way to the hospital, she took a detour by the clinic to see if any of the crew had shown up. When she saw the idle equipment, she immediately called Bryan. "Does Kevin have anyone who can run the project while he's out of commission?"

"Not that I know of. He didn't mention it last night when I visited. A couple of his men showed up as I left. He must have it under control."

"No one is here. They usually arrive around seven."

"I'm just the silent partner, Em. Sorry. Why don't you ask Kevin?"

"Because he's already a challenge to keep calm. The last thing I want to do is make him think about not meeting the deadline. I know the penalty is outrageous, and Kevin's already cut the budget to the bare necessities on this, I'm sure. His bid was so much lower than the others—he has to be taking a risk as it is."

Bryan wouldn't confirm Emily's suspicions. Not that she was surprised: the two men were as loyal as blood brothers. "He's feeling okay, isn't he? How long are you talking about?"

"A week or two, but that's if he takes it easy."

"Ouch." Bryan paused, then added, "That's going to hurt all right. Why don't you see if the crew shows up later on today. Maybe Kevin put someone in charge."

"I'll keep an eye on it, but in the meantime I have an idea, and want your opinion. Did you reach any of Kevin's family last night?"

"His mom picked up Alex at the airport, and they

got in late. They're staying at the Sodbuster Inn. Adam and the twins couldn't make it. Why?"

"Since Alex and Kevin both worked for his father's company, don't you think Alex would be willing to help Kevin with the project until Kevin is back one hundred percent?"

There was a long silence at the other end of the line.

"Bryan? What's wrong with the idea? I know Dr. Roberts isn't going to let Kevin go back on the site for a few weeks. He might be able to handle things in the office within a few days, but I'm sure they need a foreman, too. Don't they?"

"You and Kevin haven't talked a whole lot yet, have you?"

Emily felt an emptiness, realizing there was so much that Kevin hadn't shared with her. *What could be so horrible that Kevin wouldn't even ask his own brother for help?* "I know there must be more than what he's told me about the past few years, but—"

"Maybe it's for the best. It might be the perfect opportunity to let those two make amends. After all, Alex did come."

Emily stopped him. "Wait just a minute, Bryan. I need to know what happened."

"Kevin hoped to rebuild the business after his dad passed away. Alex didn't want anything to do with it, took off to fight forest fires. The family voted to shut down their dad's company." He paused. "I can't imagine Kevin is still upset about it. They've celebrated several holidays together since then, and the house is still standing."

Bryan offered to arrange a breakfast meeting between Kevin's family and Emily.

"Thanks, I'd appreciate it. It's going to be awkward enough to see them, let alone the fact that I want to ask a favor our first meeting. I need to make my rounds and see Kevin. If it won't work to meet at 8:30, page me."

Emily said a prayer that the breakfast meeting would go well. After her rounds she went to see Kevin. As she expected, he was flirting again—this time trying to convince the nurse to remove his IV so he could get back to work.

Darleen checked the IV in his hand, and pushed the stand closer to the bed. "No, Mr. MacIntyre, Dr. Roberts wants the IV left in for the rest of the day."

"But it's going to get in the way of my using the saw."

"I think that's the point, Kevin." Emily smiled and stepped into his room. "Thanks, Darleen. I'll handle this charmer." She turned to him. "You should be ashamed of yourself, trying to sweet-talk the nurses into breaking doctor's orders."

His smile was as mischievous as ever, and his eyebrows lifted as he shrugged. "Well, now, I can go right to the source of the problem. You're slowing me down here, Doc."

"Not nearly enough, obviously." She leaned over the side of the bed and gave him a chaste kiss on the cheek. "If you don't behave, I'm going to have to order round-the-clock supervision—"

"Well, now, that just might be worth it."

"—from one of the security officers. How are you feeling?" Emily smiled.

"I need to get out of here. I don't like hospitals."

She smoothed his sheets, wondering how she was ever going to convince him to slow down enough to let his body recover from the accident. "It won't be long 'til you can go home, *if* you cooperate and follow doctor's orders."

"I have a job to do, Emily. You know as well as I do what a tight schedule we're on. I can't afford to sit in here."

"I understand, and I want you back at work, too. But more important, I want to make sure you're okay." Emily gazed into his blue eyes. *I want you around forever, Kevin.* "Do you have anyone who can take over for a while?"

He laughed. "You're looking at him. I have a small operation. Until I cover the expenses for this project, I can't afford to pay a foreman. Everything rides on finishing this project on time. Can't you check me out of here? Ple-ea-se?"

Emily was torn between laughing and crying. "No, I can't, and even if I were able, I wouldn't. You need rest!"

Kevin pushed the breakfast tray aside, slid his legs over the edge of the bed and looked around the room. "Where are my clothes?"

"I took them home to wash them. Your wallet and keys are at home. I didn't think they should be left around here. Of course, the shirt's ruined. I'll bring you some clean clothes before you're dismissed."

He frowned. "You think that's going to stop me from checking out of here?"

Emily smiled. "It works on most patients."

"Smart aleck." Kevin let out a weak chuckle and let his head relax against the pillow, then tossed it aside when its plastic cover crinkled. "As long as you're going to make me stay here, could you please bring me a decent pillow from home?"

"You want me to get things...from your house?" She didn't mean to hesitate.

"Does that bother you?"

"No, I just didn't want to presume anything, I guess." She looked at her watch and realized she didn't have much time before her meeting with Kevin's mom and brother. "I have an appointment in a few minutes. You need to rest, Kevin. We'll talk later."

After a quick goodbye, Emily drove to the Sodbuster Inn. Bryan arrived just as she did. "You ready?"

She had hardly had time to think about the fact that she was going to be seeing her former potential in-laws for the first time since the broken engagement. Her main concern right now was getting Kevin to slow down for a few weeks, which meant finding someone to help during his recovery. "I was before I saw Kevin. He's ready to check himself out and go right to work at the clinic. I know something has to be done, but are you sure I should do this?"

"Bryan!" Alex bound down the stairs and offered his hand. The two men embraced. "Looks like marriage agrees with you."

"Yes, it does. I'm anxious for you to meet the family. We'll plan on you and your mom coming over for dinner tonight."

Alex turned to Emily then, and back to Bryan. "Oh, I thought for a minute that this was your wife, but—" He did a double take, and there was a glimmer of recognition in his expression.

Mrs. MacIntyre's soft voice came from somewhere behind her. "Emily?"

Emily turned toward the woman she'd been too

proud to accept help from all those years ago. "Mrs. MacIntyre, I can't tell you how sorry I was to hear about your husband."

"Thank you. What are you doing here?"

Emily had hoped Kevin had at least mentioned they were both living in the same town, though she doubted he would have mentioned they were dating yet.

Emily looked to Bryan for support, thankful suddenly that he had come along. "I'm a doctor at the clinic Kevin's company is working on."

"Well, that explains a few things, doesn't it?" Alex chuckled. "So, are you here in an official capacity?"

"Not completely." *I'm not going to hide from the truth.* "Kevin and I started seeing each other a few weeks ago, though it's not serious, yet."

"Better have that staff of yours run a few more tests on him, then, Doctor. Until that little brother of mine realizes he needs to *make* it serious, I think he has a few more priorities to get straightened out."

"Alex, stop teasing Emily." Mrs. MacIntyre put her arm around Emily in a welcoming gesture. "I hope everything works out this time. Kevin…well, Kevin wasn't quite the same without you."

Me, neither.

Emily didn't know what to say. Everything in her life had turned upside down in the last week. She had no idea how or where to start straightening it out. Especially now.

While they ate, Emily filled them in on Kevin's condition. The only thing remaining was to ask Alex to do his younger brother a favor. Why did she feel as if she were asking for the world? *They're brothers.*

Of course he'll help. Won't he? Since she didn't have brothers, she could only go on her relationship with her sisters. And she knew from experience, they wouldn't hesitate for a minute.

She glanced at Bryan, who winked. When she couldn't speak, Bryan interjected. "Alex, Emily and I have discussed an idea, and we could use your input on the matter. Emily, go ahead."

"As I said, I'm not Kevin's primary-care doctor, but I'm certain Dr. Roberts won't want Kevin working for a few weeks. You know Kevin as well as I do. That won't stop him from trying, unless he has someone capable and trustworthy to do the job in his place—someone who knows the business—who knows the way Kevin works." Her gaze met Alex's. "I'm sure you all know how much this job means to his company. There's no way he can shut down for that long."

Alex took a deep breath and leaned back in his chair. "Who-ee, gal, I thought I was the only firefighter in the family. You sure you're ready to put out *this* blaze?"

Emily's eyes grew larger and she looked at Bryan, pleading for an explanation before she finished. Silently, she prayed, *Am I doing the right thing, God?*

Bryan chuckled. "I'll take the heat if sparks start flying."

With a glance to Kevin's mother, Emily cleared her throat. "I'm not only gambling with my feelings for Kevin, here, but—" Emily stopped. She'd almost blurted out that she had a child to think of, as well. "I'm not sure this is the right thing to do, but I can't let Kevin risk losing his company."

Alex took her hand. "I came to do this job,

whether or not anyone asked. I can't think of any better way to show my support."

Emily's mouth fell open. "He already asked you?"

Alex let out a deep laugh. "Don't get happy. What's he going to do, kick me off the site? If Kevin forgives me for the past mistakes in the process, all the better. If not, at least I tried. One thing for sure, I'm not going to let him down this time."

Emily felt tears sting her eyes. "Thank you, Alex."

"You take care of my brother, and I'll take care of his business—'til he's back in shape."

Mrs. MacIntyre's soft voice broke in. "Since we're clearing the air, I'm glad you're here, Emily. I look forward to visiting again later." She looked at Alex. "I want to see Kevin. Are you ready?"

Emily didn't know how to respond. Little by little she was discovering why Kevin was so different from the man she had almost married. "I'll see you all later, I'm sure." She pulled a card from her purse. "Here's my pager number, if you need anything."

They all rose and pushed the chairs in behind them.

"Oh, I took the clothes he was wearing when the accident happened home to wash. I told him I'd bring them back later, but I'd recommend we hold off on that as long as possible. He just may go AWOL if he has any opportunity."

Bryan gave her a hug before heading off to work. "Don't give up on him, Em. You know Kevin's too stubborn to do anything the easy way."

When she visited him that night, Kevin didn't mention Alex's helping out. She decided that it was between the brothers now. Maybe they needed more time. But could the project afford to sit idle while the two made amends?

Dr. Roberts was due anytime. Kevin turned to look at the clock again and shifted in the bed, perspiration gluing his back to the mattress. It had been two days since the accident, and he had to get to work. He was tired of sticking to the bed, eating tasteless mush and being poked and monitored.

Not only that, but being around the hospital so much was obviously bothering his mother, as well. After failing to convince her he'd be okay, and that she could go on home, they finally reached a compromise. She'd keep her hospital visits short. She and Alex would stay at his house. She could stay to take care of him for a few days after he was released from the hospital.

He had to get home before she gave his bachelor pad a whole new look—one with those feminine touches that would remind him of all that was missing in his life.

Alex made regular visits early in the morning and later in the evening. What he was doing with the rest of his time, Kevin wasn't sure. In fact, he wasn't sure why Alex was still here at all. When asked, his brother mumbled something about getting too old to be jumping into flames and looking for a new job.

It was good to see him, without the past acting as a barrier.

The alarm on the IV went off, indicating the fluid was getting low. It was also a not-so-subtle reminder that he had to convince the doctor he was well enough to go home.

Emily's visits were the highlight of his day. Being on the staff, she was the only one not kicked out when visiting hours were over—the only thing that kept him from losing his mind in here. How Emily stayed so cheerful around all this pain was beyond him.

Kevin could still see the fear in her eyes when she told his mother and Alex details about the accident. She ended by telling him over and over again that he'd "better never, ever scare her like that again."

He saw the love in her every action. And it scared the daylights out of him. If anything, the accident had proven to him that no matter how much control he thought he had, in the flash of an eye, it could be taken away.

How can I do this to her? He'd seen what his father's death had done to his mother. She still couldn't handle being in a hospital. He couldn't do that to Emily.

"Pride goeth before a fall," his father used to tell him. What a time for him to think of his dad—while lying in the hospital.

He thought of him and Alex running the family business in his father's absence—

It hit him like a ton of bricks.

Alex.

That's what he's been doing all day. I've got to get out of here, get back to work before Alex shuts down my company, too.

Kevin sat up in bed and swung his bare legs over the side, trying to figure out how he was going to get to the construction site.

Alex probably has my truck, too.

"Morning, Kevin. How are you feeling?"

Dr. Roberts had rotten timing.

"Well enough to get out of here."

The doctor laughed. "Let's take one more look and see what your file says before you check yourself out of here." He looked at the chart and set it aside. "No more headaches, dizziness..."

"None," Kevin snapped.

The list of questions went on and on, adding to Kevin's irritation. "Dr. Roberts, I really need to get back to work."

He thought of his mother. Emily. Alex.

None of them had given him a clue as to what was happening in the outside world. "I have people to see. I don't have time to sit around here doing nothing."

"Now, now, Mr. MacIntyre. Let me review a few things with you."

Before Kevin knew it, he'd been sidelined for a indeterminate length of time.

In the back of his mind he heard the doctor mention seeing him in three to four days for a checkup without saying exactly how long he would have to stay away from work.

No lifting, no physical exertion, nothing.

The old codger winked. "I'd hate to have to pull the clinic contract in order to make sure you take care of yourself. Don't worry, your brother has everything running smoothly."

Kevin snapped inside, but somehow managed to remain calm on the outside. "My brother may have come to help, but I still run the project. With all due respect, I can't afford to stay off clinic property for another day."

Dr. Roberts chuckled. "Fine, but I'd better not see

you lifting even a hammer, Kevin. First it's a hammer, then the saw, then a plate-glass window. Don't push your luck. I'm serious."

Kevin laughed. Weren't all doctors always serious? *Must be an occupational hazard.*

Kevin couldn't believe that Alex filling in hadn't crossed his mind earlier. Kevin hoped he didn't look half as foolish as he felt. His brother wasn't just looking for any job; Alex was taking *Kevin's* job.

"When can I go home, Dr. Roberts?"

"I'll sign the release—shouldn't take too long. Why don't you get dressed and call a ride to get you out of here."

Kevin held out his hand. "Thanks, Doc. See you in a few days."

The doctor gripped Kevin's hand firmly and smiled. "Someone upstairs gave you a second chance. Don't take that for granted."

Nodding, he waited for the physician to finish signing the papers.

Kevin knew better than to look for his clothes—all he would find were empty closets. He'd searched for a way out yesterday, hoping Emily had put them away while he wasn't looking.

Now, not only did he need to call home for a ride, but he had to wait for his clothes to arrive, as well. When he called the house, no one was home.

He called Emily. In the background he heard pounding and sawing. "Emily, my brother is doing my job, isn't he?"

The silence lengthened, and he heard Emily close her door to the noises that were as comforting to him as a worn-out sweatshirt. "This is no time to let your stubborn pride stand in the way, Kevin."

"I want a straight answer, Emily."

"I don't know where he is right now, but yes, Kevin, Alex is making sure things continue to run smoothly with your project."

"You couldn't have told me two days ago?" he said, and failed to keep the anger from his voice.

Emily's words were tart with professionalism. "Two days ago, you were so out of it you wouldn't have understood what I was saying if I *had* told you. I thought you'd appreciate your brother's help. He's making sure the work is getting done."

"You just had to take over, didn't you?" The minute he said the words, he was sorry.

"It won't happen again."

"I'm sorry, Emily—" She'd already hung up.

Kevin closed his eyes. *Great way to make amends, Kevin.* He wove his fingers together behind his neck and lay back on the bed. *I think it's time we have a talk, God.*

An hour later his brother walked into the hospital room, carrying a change of clothes and the keys to Kevin's truck. "I understand you're not terribly happy with me."

Alex always did know how to make an entrance.

"If you wanted a job, you could have asked."

Alex nodded slightly, not looking at all remorseful or worried. "A lot less headache this way. When that old codger gives you your life back, I'll be tossed aside like a dirty shirt, and you know it."

Kevin didn't know how to deny it. Though he had forgiven his family for the decision they'd made years ago, he wasn't sure it was good business to bring "family" into the picture again. "It isn't that I—"

Alex dropped into the chair across from the table and crossed one ankle over his opposite knee. "I want to help, to tell you I'm sorry. To let you know how proud I am of you and what you're doing. You're not too proud to accept that, are you?"

He struggled with his stubborn pride, afraid of making matters with his brother worse. It wasn't that he didn't want Alex here. Admittedly, he wasn't up to speed yet, and he would have been scrambling to run the job from afar. But he was in no position to offer his brother what a foreman should earn—even temporarily.

Kevin took a deep breath and repeated the verse silently: "A friend loves at all times, and a brother is born for adversity."

"Thanks. I'll admit, I'm not at all happy with having to sit the bench on this, but if there's anyone I trust to do it right, it's you. About the pay—"

"Don't worry about it." A look of trepidation crossed Alex's face.

Kevin knew the spring thunderstorms made this the busiest season for smokejumpers, and Alex's presence here was costing him plenty. "I plan to worry about it. And I plan to pay you."

"You don't need to, okay?"

He looked suspiciously at his brother. "You dropped your job, flew down here on the spur of the moment—which couldn't have been cheap—and you don't want to be paid? What's going on, Alex?"

Kevin heard dainty footsteps enter the room.

"I paid him already, and before you start yelling,

I asked him not to say anything,'' Emily's soft voice explained. ''I wanted to help.''

He turned toward her. It was bad enough that he was incapacitated physically and facing his ex-fiancée who'd already saved his life once, but to have her taking care of his business obligations was totally out of the question, and he didn't hesitate to tell her so.

She looked at his hospital gown and back at his face. ''So, let me get this straight. It would have been okay for your parents to pay for me to go to medical school, yet I can't help you out?''

''This isn't at all the same situation, Doc. We aren't—'' He stopped short of saying they weren't committed to one another the way they had been then. ''I pay my own employees.''

She looked as if he'd just punched her, and an unwelcome tension stretched between them.

''I see.'' Emily's eyes revealed her mounting anger. ''Consider it an investment, Kevin. The sooner you finish the job, the sooner we can both move on with our lives.''

Emily whirled around and walked out of the room.

Kevin tripped over the hospital tray and headed after her, the tails of his gown flapping as he ran down the hall. She ran into the elevator, and the door closed before he could stop her.

Kevin hit the button and pounded his fist against the stainless-steel door.

''Ah, Kevin?''

''What?'' he growled. What could his brother have to say *now?*

Alex stepped behind him, tugged the back of

Kevin's gown together and whispered, "You're putting on quite a show, little brother."

Kevin turned and waved to the wide-eyed audience, furious that his brother and the hospital staff had seen him chasing after a woman—especially Dr. Emily Berthoff. "I can't wait to get out of here," he muttered.

Chapter Fourteen

Emily leaned against the wall of the elevator and closed her eyes. *You are so stubborn, Kevin!* She ran her fingers through her hair, pulling the bulk of it into a clip.

She had been fool enough to think there was a chance she could actually become whole again. That Kevin would wake up, anxious to tell her directly what he'd told Pastor Mike while in his stupor from painkillers—that he loved her.

Mike had come to visit as soon as he heard about Kevin's accident, both to pray for Kevin and to offer Emily support. They had both stayed with Kevin for most of the day. Emily was grateful that Mike had a wonderful sense of humor and already knew how Emily felt about Kevin, or it could have been quite an eye-opener when Kevin warned the pastor not to get any ideas about her. The warning had been followed by an emotionally garbled, "I love her."

It had been two days since Kevin's babbles had given her hope, only to have him dash them again in his alert, clear-minded stubbornness.

I've waited eight years to find this kind of love again, God. Why can't Kevin give us another chance?

Her pager beeped, and she pressed the button to silence it, seeing the code from the maternity ward. *Mrs. Apple's labor pains must be getting closer.* Emily took a deep breath and pushed the elevator button to return to the third floor.

A few hours later, Emily finally made it home with a bag of French fries and a burger. Katarina was home from her business trip and met her at the door.

"I thought you had the evening off."

"I filled in for Bob."

Katarina scolded her with a tip of her head. "That's the third time in the month that I've been here! Doesn't the man realize you have a life?"

"I do?" Emily said sarcastically. She moved into the living room and dropped onto the sofa. The picture of a rainbow that Ricky had drawn for her sent her back to the weekend—before Kevin's accident. Had it only been four days since she'd learned of Gretchen and Jack's request?

"What is bothering you? You haven't looked this sick since you caught the flu from Stanley What's-his-name right before Homecoming."

"Nothing's wrong with me," she said, then filled her mouth with an oversize bite of hamburger.

Katarina made a show of checking Emily's forehead for a fever. "Something *must* be wrong if you stopped at a fast-food place for dinner."

Emily forced a smile. "I'll be okay. How was your trip? I want to hear all about it." There was nothing Katarina could do to alleviate her concerns. Only Kevin could do that. And it didn't appear he was inclined to do so anytime soon. "Did you get any contracts?"

"Oh, no, no, no. Don't you change the subject." Katarina dropped into the seat next to her, pulled Emily's shoes from her feet and began massaging. "Come on, sis, spill it."

Emily collapsed against the back of the sofa and let herself relax as her sister worked the aches from her feet. *Maybe it would help just having someone to share my worries with.* "You wouldn't believe the week I've had."

She told Katarina about the turn her weekend with Ricky's grandparents had taken, and about Kevin's accident.

"You're serious. I mean, Kevin almost died?"

She tipped her head to the side in disbelief. "I'm a doctor, Kat. I don't joke about things like that."

"But he's fine now? He's thrilled to have another chance to make you blissfully happy? To be the father of your children, and Ricky?"

Emily rolled her eyes. "Where do you store all that optimism?" Her sister kneaded a knot from Emily's left arch, and Emily jerked the foot away, only to have it snatched back. "No, Kat, in fact, he's furious with me for trying to help. I can't believe I ever let myself hope it could all work out."

"Give him time."

"I don't have that luxury. Ricky doesn't, either." Emily felt the weight of the world on her shoulders. "After today, I just keep thinking how wrong I am to even consider adopting him. What would I do if I had to respond to an emergency?"

"Child care. A nanny. For now, I can certainly help watch him. There are a lot of single parents,

Emily. It's not like when Mom was trying to raise us."

"Look at my hours," Emily argued. "It's ten o'clock, and I'm just eating dinner. I couldn't do that to a little boy."

Katarina's eyebrows arched in an I-told-you-so expression. "You'd get used to cutting the day shorter. You wouldn't take others' calls quite so readily. You would have time for yourself, which, quite honestly, would be good for you. And becoming a mother would be a wonderful excuse that no one would argue with."

Emily looked at her sister longingly. She wished she had even one-fourth the enthusiasm her sister did. "Mother should have named you Pollyanna. How do you even make decisions? You can't possibly look at both sides of a problem."

"Usually the negative is already in front of me. That leaves me to focus on the positive. Which is what I want you to do. Think of three reasons why you *should* adopt Ricky. You obviously feel something more for him than for your typical patient, or you'd already have said no."

Emily thought of the adorable little boy. That was the easy part. But a child's adorableness was no reason to adopt. She needed a better motive.

He needed love.

He is so lovable. Yes, she could easily love Ricky. *I could love a dog, too, but I don't have one.*

"Ricky will have a lot of emotions to deal with."

Kat tickled the bottom of Emily's toes, and Emily felt her body relax.

"Turning that one around to fulfill the requirements, Doctor, you would need to add 'And who better to help him than me?' After all, you do have the training."

Emily frowned. "I'm not a psychiatrist."

"Never stopped you from giving advice before. Now, think of a positive reason."

Pulling her pampered feet from her sister's lap, Emily sat up. "Don't you have something else to do?"

Katarina rubbed her hands along her blue jeans and crossed them in front of her. "Nothing. Get busy thinking. Come on, think positive."

After trying to sort out her feelings, Emily finally came up with one she really wasn't sure should qualify. "I want a family?"

Katarina smiled. "Good."

"But I have such a demanding career, horrible hours. And what would I ever do about being on call?"

Her sister's animated groan almost made Emily laugh. "Oh, no, and I thought you were actually going to come up with one."

Katarina looked at Emily as if she were some forlorn old maid whose days were numbered. "Your career is your life because you let it be. You knew you wanted a family when you decided to become a doctor. You knew there would come a time when you would eagerly make time for a husband and children."

"Which is another point. I'm single."

Katarina sighed. "Having two parents doesn't guarantee happiness *or* a good family life. You have so much to offer a child, Emily. Besides, what happens if you never meet Mr. Right?"

How could Katarina even think such a thing? In

the back of her mind, Emily thought of Kevin. She recalled the way he had looked in a suit, romping on the floor with Jacob and Laura's children.

He denied wanting children, even though he was wonderful with them and at one time wanted a houseful. She and Kevin were just now beginning to work things out, and adding a child would throw a definite wrench into the works. She hoped that one day Kevin would change his mind and realize what he was missing. *Surely he'll change his mind.*

"I could lose Kevin if I choose to adopt Ricky."

"That's not at all positive, Emily! You're thinking of this all wrong. I hate to break my own rule, but I will, for Ricky's sake." Her voice lowered. "If Kevin leaves because you have a child, it was never meant to be in the first place, and Ricky would save you another huge mistake. You wouldn't truly be happy, even with Kevin, if you sacrificed a family for marriage."

The gaze in her sister's eyes was sympathetic, silently sharing the misery of the truth.

"I think you missed your calling, Kat. I think you should be the psychiatrist."

Her sister pushed herself to her feet and shrugged. "Not me! That's way too serious. By the way, Kevin called while you were at the hospital. He asked you to return the call when you got home."

Emily tried to tame the glimmer of hope before it consumed her again. She watched her sister head toward the stairs. "Oh, Kat. Don't mention Ricky to anyone, please. I need some time to make a decision."

"As long as you need me, Em, I'm here. Remember that."

Emily smiled. She knew she could count on her sister.

"I can do all things through Christ who strengthens me." I believe You, God, but I can't do it alone. Help me make the best decision for Ricky.

She called Kevin, prepared for the worst yet hoping for the best. Emily took a deep breath. She hadn't meant to interfere with his business. She'd wanted to help. To show him that he was important to her. They had both been through so much recently, it was no wonder tempers were flaring.

Kevin answered immediately. "Emily, I'm so sorry I yelled at you. I'm not handling any of this well. It hit me so unexpectedly. I appreciate your help, and—I'll pay you back, if you want to consider it..."

She couldn't answer.

"Are you there?"

"Uh-huh. I don't consider it a loan, so we don't need to bring it up again. I gave it because I wanted to, and I would really like it if you'd simply learn to accept help graciously."

The deep timbre of Kevin's voice faded to a low whisper. "Thank you."

Emotion caught in her throat. Relief wasn't far behind. She took a drink of water and tried to compose herself.

"I didn't mean to make you cry." He paused. "You're supposed to save those for when I'm there to dry them, don't you know?"

Emily laughed at his unexpected advice. "I didn't know you were so fond of tears. Been breaking a lot of hearts, have you?"

"Only one that matters."

She couldn't speak. Her heart beat faster. The tears started again. It had been so long since she'd let herself care for anyone. Emily decided God had other plans for her life, after all. "I'd better go, Kevin. I'm sorry."

"It's okay, Emmy. I hate to admit it, but I am tired. Looks like I'm going to have some free time tomorrow, if you can get away for lunch or something."

"I have the day off. Why don't you let me fix you and your mother lunch."

"That sounds great. We'll see you then. Sweet dreams, Doc."

"You, too." Emily went to bed, hope blanketing her in warmth. Her thoughts drifted to Ricky, and she wondered how he was doing. She was ashamed to realize she hadn't called him once since Kevin's accident. She jotted a note, reminding herself to call him first thing in the morning on the pad next to her phone.

Emily pulled her Bible from the shelf and opened her study guide for the first time in a week. It seemed a lifetime ago. She read the lesson from the day of Kevin's accident, and paused. "'I will not leave you as orphans; I will come to you,'" she read in a whisper, then read it again.

Emily called Ricky first thing the next morning and visited. He sounded happy and seemed to be enjoying his "visit," as he called it. She was relieved. When his grandparents got on, she explained why she hadn't called sooner. His grandparents sent him next door then, and bragged about about how well Ricky was adjusting to his parents' death.

"We can thank Laura for that. She's had a lot of experience answering little ones' questions about death." Emily sipped her orange juice and jotted down a few more things to pick up at the grocery store.

George suggested Emily plan for Ricky to come spend a couple of weeks with her. They were enjoying their grandson, but were wearing out already. Emily looked at her calendar, and promised to come pick him up in a week and a half.

"Have you made any decision yet, Emily?"

She sighed. "No. I adore Ricky, but I'm just not sure I am the best person for the job. I look at this week and wonder how a child would have fit into that."

"I'm sure it's very difficult for you, and we don't want to pressure you. Really we don't—" George's voice broke. "If you don't think you can take him, we really need to start looking for the right family. He's been through so many changes already. I want him to get settled soon. Harriet's not doing well."

Emily rubbed her forehead. "I understand." After asking about Harriet's health, she added, "I'll be in touch soon, George." Emily hung up and immediately thought of the verse in her study last night.

As soon as she composed herself again, Emily went to the store and picked up steak and vegetables to make fajitas. After slicing the meat, she put it in the bowl with the marinade, then cut up the peppers, onion and tomatoes and set them in the refrigerator, her mind still on the conversation with George.

She tossed a salad, annoyed by the steady drip of water from the faucet. While setting the table, Emily turned on the stereo, hoping the music would drown out the noise. The rhythms were out of synchronization, and it only made matters worse. "How long has this faucet been dripping, Kat?"

"A few days, I guess. I meant to call a plumber before my trip, but didn't get around to it."

"Probably needs a washer tightened or something. It'll take forever for a repairman to get here. That's going to drive me insane with company here." Emily went to the drawer, pulled out the pliers and tried to tighten a nut that went around the base of the faucet. The drip got worse. "Oh, come on. Don't do this now."

"I have a meeting with a Realtor. I'll see you later."

Emily offered her halfhearted best wishes to Kat on finding a studio that had room for a few employees and storage for her stock. The door closed behind her sister as Emily pried the cover off the handle and started turning the screwdriver. *Maybe if I readjust the handle, it'll make it through lunch, anyway.*

"Morning, beautiful. I saw Katarina outside, and she told me to come on in." Kevin closed the door and walked across the living room. "What are you doing?"

Emily turned, relieved to see Kevin. "Hi. Where's your mother?"

"She thought we should have some time alone after..." He stepped closer. "You're not taking that off, are you?"

"I'm just going to see if the washer needs to be replaced."

"You did shut off the main water valve, didn't..."

Emily lifted the screw out and jiggled the handle, and the water exploded like a fountain all over the kitchen. "Help!" She tried to put the handle back on, which only made matters worse.

"Move. Hold a bowl or pan over that so it will at least force it back into the sink." Kevin dropped to the ground, pushing her aside. He reached under the sink, tossing bottles of cleaner out of his way. He let out a grunt, then yelled, "Wrench!"

She grabbed the pliers and handed them to him. He popped his head out of the cabinet and gave her a look of disgust.

She shrugged her shoulders. "It's all I have."

Groaning, he banged on the handle and began twisting. "Give me some oil. Maybe that'll loosen this rust."

Emily looked at the pan, knowing that the minute she let go of it, water would spray everywhere again. At least his idea kept it somewhat contained. "It's in the cabinet across the kitchen, to the right of the stove. Can you get it? If I move, the water's going to spray everywhere again."

Emily looked at the pictures on her refrigerator that were ruined, the Victorian lace curtains that were dripping water, and the puddles inching their way toward the carpet.

He scooted across the floor and returned with the towel and oil. A few minutes later, the water finally slowed to a stop. Kevin slid out of the cabinet again and slumped against the refrigerator. "You forgot one itty-bitty detail, Doc."

"Sorry."

Kevin laughed. He looked at her and smiled. "What was that agreement we made? I won't practice medicine, you don't do any building? Let's add plumbing to that list."

Soaked, Emily knelt next to him and lifted one eyebrow. "Don't suppose I could beg for mercy and ask you for a favor?"

He pulled her into his soggy embrace. "Gee, I don't know. You haven't saved my life, or my business, or...anything." His words faded into a whisper as he gave her a kiss that made her very happy she was already sitting down.

Chapter Fifteen

The next morning, Kevin discussed the clinic plans with Alex, answering his questions about the next phase of the project. Kevin struggled over leaving his "baby" in someone else's hands, though he knew Alex was more than capable of handling everything. Throughout the first week, he made excuses to stop in daily. Kevin soon realized everything was under control and that he might as well get other work done.

Knowing the project was back on track made it easier for him to follow doctors' orders—both Emily's and Dr. Roberts's. The last thing he wanted was *more* medical attention.

With any luck at all, Monday morning the doctor would give him the all-clear to return to work next week.

Taking advantage of Alex's help, Kevin prepared bids for future projects and caught up on paperwork. After looking at the stack of potential contracts, Kevin ran a few figures through the computer, and smiled. He was beginning to see real benefits to having his brother around.

Despite his initial anger, the two were working well together, and Kevin was beginning to wonder if there was room to add *Brothers* to the name MacIntyre Construction, after all. If Alex was serious about giving up firefighting, he and his brother had something to discuss.

Kevin stopped by the clinic to check on the progress the crew had made under Alex's sole direction. He had to admit, the results were impressive. Still, though they were back on schedule without him and he'd been relieved to get ahead on the office work, Kevin was itching to get his hands dirty again.

Kevin walked inside, greeting the staff along the way. As he got closer to Emily's office, he overheard Bob Walker trying to sweet-talk her again.

"I had a small mix-up for this weekend, Em. I didn't realize it was my turn to be on call already, and I made other plans. Could you fill in for me?" the man begged.

Emily didn't respond. Kevin peeked around the corner, trying to decide whether to walk on in or wait in the hall. A smile remained plastered painfully to her bright face. She was going to give in, again.

Oh, no, you don't, Doc. If you're too generous to say no, then I'll take care of it for you.

Kevin stepped into the room, startling both Emily and the other doctor. "Hi, sweetheart, sorry I'm late. I just picked up our train tickets for this weekend. It's all planned. Hot springs, here we come."

"Kevin!" Her green eyes widened in amazement when he wrapped his arm around her and kissed her on the cheek, then turned to the arrogant Dr. Walker and smiled.

The man's face went blank as he stammered, "I—I didn't think you'd be busy. Sorry. You and the builder are...?"

"Very close," Kevin confirmed, hugging Emily.

"Oh, Kevin and me? Yes, we go way back." She looked up at him with "I can't believe you did this" twinkling in her eyes.

Bob backed slowly away. "I didn't realize. Well, if you'll excuse me. Ah, have a nice weekend."

"Same to you, Bob," Kevin said, loosening his hold on Emily.

She was still gazing up at him, but said to Dr. Walker, "Sorry I can't cover for you again, Bob."

"I'll figure something out." The man backed out of the office, his stare boring through Kevin as he turned around.

"I'm sure you will." How she managed to sound sweet was beyond Kevin's comprehension.

Kevin watched to make sure Bob was out of earshot, then closed the door. He studied her sanctuary lined with medical books and journals. There was nothing in here that revealed the Emily he had once loved, just the doctor she had become. Her many honors lined the walls of her study. *Summa cum laude,* Johns Hopkins School of Medicine. Fellowship, American Academy of Obstetrics... Kevin turned away from the reminders of what had come between them and what it had already cost them.

"Why didn't you just tell the jerk 'no'?"

"I was going to, before you interrupted with that *outrageous* claim of yours. And where in the world did you come up with 'sweetheart'? Good grief,

Kevin. Do you realize the implications?'' she asked with quiet emphasis.

His blue eyes narrowed speculatively. ''I would have thought that removing yourself as my physician would already have opened up the 'implication' file.''

''The only one who knows—make that *knew*, was Dr. Roberts. But that's obviously not the case now. Everyone will know by Monday morning.''

''I'm tired of watching you work yourself into the ground. Don't you ever take time to relax?''

Emily tilted her head to the side and placed one hand on her hip. ''Aren't you one to talk? If you weren't working all the time, you wouldn't know how many hours I put in, now would you?''

He didn't bother pointing out that he'd just taken time ''off,'' since, just as soon as he was able, he'd be making her statement true again. ''So we both work too much, which is all the more reason we need to get out of town.''

''I hope you enjoy yourself,'' Emily said absently as she stepped behind the desk to the chair and opened a patient file.

Kevin saw the phone book standing on her desk and looked up a number, while Emily returned to her work. He reached for the receiver and dialed a number. ''Yes, I'd like to see if you can reserve two tickets for the train ride to Glenwood tonight.'' He smiled. ''Great, I'll be right over to pay. My name is Kevin MacIntyre.''

Emily popped back to her feet. ''You wouldn't dare.''

Kevin looked at the phone and handed it to her. ''I just did. We're going to relax if it kills us. I might as well take a few days to get away while Alex is still around, right? Can you be ready at five?"

Emily thought of Ricky. He'd be arriving next weekend, and she had to get a room ready for his visit. Even though it was officially just a visit, she was thinking of it as—sort of a trial run—and she wanted everything to be just right. "I can't go."

He leaned over and kissed her cheek, whispering in her ear, "The break will be good for both of us. We haven't had much time together. I think it's time we do, don't you?"

Emily felt her heart skip a beat. "Oh, Kevin. I don't know." She felt the blood rush to her cheeks. He sounded so—serious.

She thought of Ricky, and becoming a mother, and the fact that this might be her last chance to get away, as well. Though Katarina claimed she'd be willing to continue living with her in order to make the transition smooth, Emily was still hesitant. *If I adopt Ricky, I'm going to have to rethink* everything *I do.*

His gaze bore into her in silent expectation. Before she knew it, Kevin was standing next to her and lifting her chin to him. When he spoke, his voice was tender. "Come on, Emily. With our careers, you never know how long it might be before we have the chance to get away again."

Suddenly the distance between them faded, and Emily could think of only one reason to stay home—fear.

A lot had changed since they had been engaged. "Older and wiser" was more than just a quaint phrase to her—it was what had given her the courage to accept God's forgiveness and rededicate herself to Him. *You have to talk to Kevin before it's too late.*

Two hours later, Kevin drove up to the house and knocked on the door. He loaded her bag into the truck for the short drive to Union Station in Denver to catch the train.

Once the truck door closed and they pulled away from the curb, Kevin took her hand. "I want to give it another try, Emmy."

For the past two hours she'd practiced how to tell him there was someone else in her life that was now her first priority. She took a deep breath, yet her courage faltered. *Give me the words to tell him, Father.* Would he understand why it had to be different between them this time?

"What makes you think anything has changed, Kevin? If anything, we're even more set in our own lives now."

"Hasn't this past month been enough to show you that we can juggle schedules with the rest of this crazy world? Before my accident, I didn't think I could let Alex help with the business, either, and that's working fine." Kevin told her in detail about the disagreement between Alex and him that had led to closing down his father's business. Until Alex had come here, the two men had simply ignored the issue, finding that the only way to get along.

"I realize now that life is too short to harbor anger and bitterness, Emily." He paused, then added with quiet emphasis, "I don't have time for it."

Hope took another step up the ladder to her dreams.

If he could allow himself to change in that respect, maybe he could eventually change his mind about a future for the two of them, and a family to fulfill all of their dreams.

"I've spent my time off in my office, preparing bids, and filling out contracts. God's been good to me. I'm going to have to hire help to keep up with everything if I want a life at all."

He went on excitedly about his hopes of asking his brother to stay on permanently, and eventually expanding to two totally separate divisions.

Emily was thrilled to see Kevin's excitement over the changes Alex's presence had made. They pulled off the interstate and turned into the Friday evening rush-hour traffic. Kevin unplugged his car phone and stashed it in the glove box. "Do you want something to eat before we get to the station?"

She shook her head. "I'm fine, but feel free to get something if you want." The opportunity to get into a new discussion had passed, she realized.

Traffic moved like molasses on a winter day, and Kevin pulled into the first burger joint they saw. "We may as well eat something while we sit in the traffic. I know you're not fond of junk food, but they do make a great bowl of chili."

She smiled. "That sounds good. Here, let me." Emily pulled a bill from her purse.

"I thought we covered this already." He quirked his eyebrow.

"So did I," she said, gently reminding him of the conversation they had had the previous week about the joy of giving, and learning to receive graciously. "I didn't argue when you made the reservations for both of us, did I? Well, not too hard, anyway."

He placed the order and accepted the twenty. "Thank you for dinner." She didn't fail to notice the note of resignation in his voice.

"You're welcome. And thank you for making me

take time to relax.'' Emily tried to keep her own tone playful.

Finally the traffic thinned, and they were able to find a parking spot at Union Station. After checking their luggage, they boarded the train. Emily sat next to Kevin, feeling snug and comfortable. Conversing quickly became awkward over the noise of other passengers. The rhythm of the train ride was strangely relaxing. Emily fell asleep with her head resting on Kevin's shoulder and didn't wake until they pulled into the station at Glenwood.

The shuttle driver met them inside the small station to take them to the hotel. Emily and Kevin found their bags and climbed into the van. Immediately offended by one of the young men whose breath smelled like the inside of a beer barrel, Emily leaned closer to Kevin.

Kevin wrapped his arm protectively around her shoulder. ''We should be there soon.''

A few minutes later the driver pulled up in front of the historic Rockfront Inn. Kevin grabbed their luggage from the back and escorted Emily to the registration desk. ''Why don't you pick up a few brochures, see if you can find something fun for us to do tomorrow. I'm taking care of this,'' Kevin whispered.

She started to speak, then saw the look of reproach in his gaze. Reluctantly, Emily glanced at the advertisements, picked up a few that looked interesting and waited for Kevin to return.

''We're on the second floor. The pool is closed for tonight, but opens at ten in the morning.'' With Kevin leading, they climbed the wide stairs and turned left.

Emily paused momentarily to admire an antique chest in the hallway. Kevin set their bags in front of a door and inserted the key.

I have to say something, she thought.

"Here you go." Kevin opened the door and motioned her inside.

Her feet were like lead. She dragged herself into the room and looked around. Her stomach churned with anxiety. Though she was relieved that he'd reserved a two-room suite, she still had to make a few things clear. The door closed at the other end of the room, and Emily panicked.

"Kevin, we can't share a room," she blurted out, rushing on before she lost her courage. "There's someone more important in my life now—"

Emily spun around. The room was empty.

"Kevin?" She searched the bedroom, the bathroom, the closet. No one.

She ran to the door and opened it. Across the hall, the door opened and Kevin stepped out.

"How's your room?" He gave her an irresistibly devastating grin, and she knew she'd been set up.

"You...are so ornery!" The tension broke, and Emily began laughing.

The smile in his eyes contained a sensuous flame. He lifted her room key and quirked a brow questioningly. "May I? I'd like to explain, in private."

Emily took the key defiantly and crossed her arms in front of her. "I don't know," she teased. "I'm not very happy that you made me agonize over this for the last six hours."

"Forgive me?" His brilliant blue eyes sparked with excitement. "I wanted to see how much you trusted me."

"Now you're testing me?"

"Us." Kevin took her by the shoulders and pulled her close, his gaze as soft as a caress. "Testing us," he whispered. He paused as if asking for permission before his mouth covered hers.

A few moments lost in the velvety warmth of his kiss, and all the emotions of their past returned. The warmth of his embrace was so male, so comforting. Emily wanted the moment to last forever. Kevin leaned against the wall, holding her firmly against him as the kiss ended.

Emily opened her eyes, drinking in the sight of him. A small one-inch scar from the accident was all that was left to remind her that she'd almost lost him. Tentatively, she reached up and touched the tender skin on Kevin's chin.

Kevin jumped slightly, releasing his hold on her, both emotionally and physically. "It's late. Why don't we talk tomorrow." His voice was low and ragged.

Emily felt her own control wavering, and appreciated Kevin's wise decision. "Call when you wake up." She kissed him again, then backed out of his embrace, turned and opened her door.

Chapter Sixteen

Kevin was amazed that he had had the control to walk away. He opened his suitcase and took his shaving kit to the tiny bathroom. There he looked at his reflection in the mirror, focusing on the scar that had drawn Emily's attention. He knew what she had been thinking—the same thing he did every so often: he'd almost died. His finger touched the mark, bringing to mind the reality that even his own days were numbered.

After that kiss, he had thought he was protecting her, but as he lay in bed trying to sleep, he realized it was himself that he was guarding. He was afraid of losing her. Once had been torture, but to think of going through that again was more than he could comprehend.

The next morning, Kevin awoke and showered. It was still too early to take the chance of waking her, and he made a pot of the complimentary coffee included with the room. He turned on the television and occupied the time mourning the degeneration of Saturday morning cartoons.

When he called Emily's room, there was no answer. He left a message. A few minutes later she returned the call, saying she'd gone for her morning walk.

"Why didn't you call? I've been waiting to call because I thought it was too early. I'd have gone with you."

"I hoped you were getting some rest, I guess. I try to walk every morning. It's my chance to start the morning on the right foot." They decided to walk down the street for breakfast, then tour some of the historical sites in town. While they ate, Emily told Kevin little bits about her visit with Ricky's grandparents. She was tempted to tell him that she was named to be Ricky's guardian, but still she hesitated.

She'd convinced herself that it was her decision solely, that it couldn't be based upon what happened with her relationship with Kevin, or anyone else. While she would love to have someone else she could talk to about the situation, her sister's persuasion made it clear that the more opinions she sought, the more muddied the waters would become. She couldn't take any more pressure. It was something she had to trust God to help her answer in His own time. She only hoped that happened soon enough to suit Ricky's grandparents.

After shopping the morning away, they visited Doc Holliday's grave, had lunch, then stopped in to see the vapor caves before returning to the hotel.

Throughout the day, there had been an undercurrent of tension that became stronger as they approached the hotel. "Why don't we meet down at the pool," she suggested.

"You sure? We have a lot to talk about, Emily."

"After that kiss last night, I have a feeling it would be better if we avoid being alone. Hopefully we can find a quiet corner of the pool to have our visit."

His blue eyes brimmed with passion and understanding. Awkwardly, Kevin nodded, and they both escaped into the retreat of their own rooms.

Twenty minutes later, Kevin knocked on Emily's door, and the two of them walked to the pool together.

Keeping her voice low, she said, "I want to thank you for not presuming we'd continue from where we left off eight years ago, Kevin." She wasn't sure if that was a promising sign or not, but she knew it was right.

"I couldn't do that to you. I'm sure it was as difficult on you as it was me when we broke up last time. I want to be sure before we make that decision."

Emily took his hand and looked into his eyes. "With your charm, you make your restraint as flattering as a full seduction."

"I'm not trying to be charming, Emmy. I mean it. I care too much about you to hurt you again."

His smile showed the agony he, too, was feeling.

They reached the lobby and separated long enough to enter the pool area through the segregated locker rooms. After the required shower, they met on the other side and stepped into the two-block-long hot springs pool.

Emily had pulled her hair into a bun atop her head.

She dipped into the water, clear up to her chin. It felt like a soothing massage on her tired legs.

"Now this ought to work off some of that work-related tension!" Emily looked at Kevin. "Wanna race?"

He smiled. "To that shady corner. Looks quiet there."

Emily looked to the corner he was referring to, squinting. "You've got to be kidding me! That's like a marathon."

"Are you forfeiting? Too tough for you?" The laughter in his eyes was a refreshing sight.

Emily turned and started swimming, knowing she would need every advantage available. She felt Kevin's hand around her ankle, and he tugged her backward while he took the lead.

Halfway to the goal, she reached over and reciprocated. It was obvious he wasn't half as interested in winning as having a relaxing swim. He could have beaten her with both hands tied behind his back.

Finally they both reached the end and grabbed hold of the edge. "I forgot how much more tiring it is to swim in warm water," he groaned.

"Yeah, that's my problem." Between the altitude, the heat, and her own foolishness for actually trying to win, Emily was light-headed. "I need to get out for a few minutes." She climbed out, staggered to the chairs, and collapsed into the curves of the chaise longue.

Kevin grabbed two towels from the towel stand and sat down next to her. "Next time you decide to swoon, let me know ahead of time, would you?" He laughed. "You okay?"

She rolled her eyes and tossed her head back.

"I've never had this reaction to hot water before you came back into my life."

Kevin snapped the towel open and covered her. "It's still a bit chilly."

"Speak for yourself."

"I'm going to go get us something to drink. I'll be right back."

Emily watched him walk away, acutely aware of his athletic physique. His shoulders were already more tanned than her own arms, and summer hadn't even started. When he returned, she studied his face, imagining Ricky all grown up and looking just like the man in front of her.

"Do you want orange juice or grape? I had to tell them you nearly fainted to get them to let me bring the bottles out here, so you'd better make a good show of drinking one of them."

She chose the orange juice. Kevin sat down and guzzled his grape juice in silence.

"What are you thinking about?" she asked.

"I'm not the same man you walked away from eight years ago—and much as I hate to say it, I'm probably not the man you need now."

If she didn't know him so well, she would have found him almost convincing.

"I have a business that takes a lot of time, and that isn't bound to improve if I expand the company."

"I don't believe that, or we wouldn't be here now. I don't think you do, either." Emily dragged in a deep breath of the thin mountain air.

She shaded her eyes from the late-day sunshine. "I'm not the same woman you loved, either, Kevin. There's someone else in my life whose love is more important to me than anything. It was His love that carried me through the years without you."

Kevin sat up, straddling the chaise longue. He looked at her, pain filling his gaze. "That's just it, Emily. You had that one love, and I spent eight years running from Him. Until I saw how Laura's love changed Bryan, my conquests were about as far from what God wanted of me as they could have been."

Emily reached over and placed her cool hand against his cheek. "We all have things in our past we want to forget, Kevin. I'm not condemning you. I just want you to know that my relationship with God is even more important to me now than it was before. I loved you, and it was beautiful. But it was nothing compared to what it could be once God is part of both of us."

"He is, Emily. But it still isn't easy to change everything all at once." Kevin heard voices behind them and turned to see a family set down their towels. The kids ran and jumped into the water. "We're here, together. What more do you want?"

Emily couldn't believe what she was hearing. It was like riding a roller coaster. "Why did you ever make your way back into my life? You could have used *any* project to launch your commercial career, so don't give me that line again."

He closed his eyes and shook his head. Maybe she was right. Maybe deep inside, he had once hoped they could try again. Unfortunately, he had enough honor left in him to know that he couldn't take a chance on hurting her. There were plenty of ways he could have handled things when his life fell apart, but he'd run away from God and even shunned his own morals. Admitting as much to the only woman he'd truly loved would only hurt her more. He couldn't lie to Emily, and he couldn't tell her the truth. He had to walk away now, before it was too late.

Kevin stood up and gathered his towel.

"Don't even think of leaving here without giving me an answer, Kevin James MacIntyre." She felt her voice crack, felt herself losing control. She couldn't do this. She couldn't let him walk away again. Something had hurt him. She had to know what had changed the man she loved. The only man she would ever love.

"I didn't come to Springville for you, Emily!" He raked his hands through his hair and took hold from the roots. "Or to prove anything to you. And especially not to hurt you. Yet that's all I've done. You deserve better." He hesitated before meeting her gaze.

"What's that supposed to mean?" Emily rose from the chair and stepped closer, lowering her voice. "You brought me here, Kevin." She wondered if he understood the reference to the resort where he had planned to surprise her on their honeymoon. "Why?"

"For some R and R. I'm tired of that jerk taking advantage of your generosity!"

"You could have done that *any* place. It didn't have to be here."

A faintly uncomfortable look of understanding flashed in his eyes. "I didn't realize you knew," he quietly admitted.

"The hotel called the day after our—when we never showed up. You weren't at home, so they tracked me down, somehow."

Kevin dropped into the cushioned sofa. "It was a lousy idea, coming here. You have dreams I can't share anymore."

Dare she hope he would change his mind? Could she convince him that there was hope for a future together? It felt so right telling Dr. Casanova that she and Kevin had plans. It felt right accepting his invitation. It felt right being here with him.

Despite her inner turmoil, she had known all along that she still loved Kevin. But was their love strong enough to heal the pain that had cost him his dreams?

"I had hopes that your bringing me here was a positive sign." She moved next to him and brushed his smooth cheek. Kevin pushed her hand away.

"I'm not going to have this discussion out here."

"Fine, Kevin. Go on up. I'll call when I'm dressed."

Kevin went on ahead, and Emily waited. She took her time, wanting some space to think without the temptation of Kevin's nearness.

Emily showered, anxious to rinse the drying minerals off her skin and out of her hair. When she was dressed, she went to Kevin's room, surprised to see that it was tiny, with only a bed and chair.

"Do you mind if we go downstairs for dinner first?"

"Yes, Kevin, I do mind." Emily turned, opened her door again, and walked in and sat down on the sofa, struggling with the sudden uncertainty that had been wakened between them.

She recalled his proclamation of love while he'd been taking the strong painkillers, and longed to hear those words again, ungarbled and clear-minded this time.

Emily placed her arm on the back of the sofa.

Kevin squirmed away, forcing a smile. ''Don't do this, Emmy. I...want you in my life. I don't want to, but I do.''

''I know. I feel the same way.'' She moved away. The harder she tried to deny the truth, the more it persisted. She couldn't hold her feelings inside any longer. ''I love you, Kevin.''

Their eyes met, and Kevin's smile disappeared. ''This was a mistake.'' He jumped up, his long gait carrying him quickly to the door. ''Do us both a favor. Lock the door behind me.''

Emily hugged her legs to her chest and rested her head on her knees. *God, I can't do this alone. I can't stop loving him. I can't change him, but I can't let him give up, either.* She let the silent tears fall, and listened to the door bang on the other side of the hall.

Several minutes later, she stood and crossed the empty hotel room, locking the door on her way to the kitchenette. As she opened the tiny refrigerator, she heard a quiet knock on the door. Emily set the apple on the counter and tentatively walked to the entrance to put her eye to the peephole.

It was black. Someone was holding a hand over the glass.

She paused. ''Take your hand off the peephole.'' She waited a second, then looked again. It was Kevin, his head drooping as if he'd lost his best friend.

''I have one more thing to say, Emily. Please give me just a minute.''

She opened the door, praying that it would be the last barrier between them.

He stood, hands braced against the doorjambs. "I can't predict the outcome, Emily. I've spent eight years learning to block out all the emotions you've brought back to life in a matter of weeks."

"I hope you don't expect me to apologize for that."

He wrapped her in his arms and held her. "Part of me wants to thank you, and the other is just too plain scared to do anything. It's not fair to move on to the next level until we've made that promise. I won't put us through that again. You have my word."

Emily's body relaxed against him. "Whether you like it or not, Kevin, you are my dream come true."

"I'm not worthy of your love, but I'm selfish enough to take it." Wrapping one arm tightly around her, he gave her a kiss that she wouldn't soon forget. Then he turned, walked across the hall to his own room and locked his door.

Two hours later, there was a knock on the door, followed by "Room service."

Suspicious, Emily looked out the peephole again. On the table was a bouquet of wildflowers and two dinner trays.

"I'm afraid you have the wrong room."

"Is this Dr. Emily Berthoff's suite?"

She placed a hand on her hip. "Yes, but I didn't order anything. Possibly it belongs across the hall."

Kevin's voice interrupted. "I'll take care of this."

She opened the door a crack, and saw Kevin tip the man. Kevin placed his hands on the table and looked up at her. "Would you like some dinner?"

She opened the door. "You told me to lock the door. I trusted you meant it."

He looked like a broken man. "You bring out the best and the worst in me, Emily."

She smiled. "Not much has changed, after all, then, has it?"

"I don't know if you're willing to take another chance..."

For a long moment she stared back at him, waiting for him to finish the suggestion. He didn't. "I am."

Kevin stepped around the table, then brought two chairs over; he held one out for her to be seated.

She looked at the elegant table, then at their jeans and sweatshirts. "I feel underdressed."

A mischievous grin was the immediate response. "Don't go there, Emmy. The dining room downstairs is formal. That's why I ordered it for the room."

She smiled back. "And the flowers...I don't think those come complimentary with a meal, do they?" As she spoke, she leaned forward to smell them. "They're gorgeous."

"They pale in comparison to you."

Emily sipped her water. "Kevin..."

"I wanted this trip to be special, Emily. And I guess deep inside, I did choose it because it seemed like an appropriate place to pick up from where we left off, so to speak." He hesitated. "Not completely, mind you."

Her heart raced. "Right, we've talked about that." Emily felt the color rise to her cheeks.

"Emily." Kevin took her hand, and paused.

The suspense was making her dizzy all over again. Tears welled in the corners of her eyes.

Kevin jumped to his feet, ran to the bathroom and returned with a handful of tissues to dry her tears.

Kneeling beside her chair, he dabbed at her cheeks. "Emmy, I haven't even said anything yet."

She blinked. "Then say something!"

He smiled. "After all these years, you're still the one I want to share my life with. You're the only one I'll ever want."

She watched the play of emotions on his face and felt his hand gently brush her tears away again.

"Will you marry me?"

Emily gasped. "Yes, yes, yes." She wrapped her arms around him, her hands shaking, her breathing much too quick. "Ooh," she squealed. In one forward motion, she was in his arms, and the two crashed to the floor. She drank in the sweetness of his kiss.

Suddenly Kevin pulled away. "Dinner's getting cold," he said as he unwrapped her arms from his neck. "We'd better back off while we can."

She smiled, understanding too well the dangerous emotions sparking between them. They sat back in their chairs, and Kevin took her hand and bowed his head.

The full impact of his proposal hit when she opened her tray and found an engagement ring.

But her vision was filled with a mental image of sweet Ricky. She looked again at the ring, then up at Kevin. Though she thought of Ricky, something cautioned her not to ask.

"Emily? What's wrong?"

His ability to understand her silent messages unnerved her. She chose her words carefully. "Kevin, I want nothing more than to spend the rest of my life with you."

"But...?"

Tears blurred her vision. "I can't be content with half a dream. I want it all—marriage, children and my career."

He sighed heavily, and a new anguish seared her heart.

He asked, "Can't we knock down one wall at a time?"

Chapter Seventeen

Emily had put on a brave face with Kevin, determined to give him time to think about what she'd told him. Though she hadn't made a final decision about adopting Ricky, she knew Katarina was right: Emily could never settle for less.

Kevin was given permission by his doctor to resume working. As indecisive as a child in a candy store, he didn't know what he wanted to do first. Emily traded her on-call schedule with Dr. Roberts, which would give her two weeks off while Ricky was visiting.

Between their two schedules, the only meal they managed together was Friday. Emily picked up burgers for herself, Kevin and Alex, and came along when they drove to Denver to trade a door of the wrong size that had been mistakenly delivered. When they returned, Kevin and Alex were determined to install it before forecasted thunderstorms made another mess of a deadline.

The next morning, Emily and Katarina went to

Wyoming to bring Ricky for his visit. Emily was astonished by the joy that consumed her when she wrapped her arms around him and felt the strength of his embrace.

They spent the afternoon with his grandparents, then stuffed as many of Ricky's belongings in the trunk as would fit.

It was late when they pulled into Emily's driveway and unloaded. Ricky had taken a nap as they drove and wasn't ready for bed until after ten. He ran into "his" room, and up and down the stairs, despite reminders not to run in the house.

When she and Kevin finally had a chance to talk in private, it was nearly midnight. Kevin suggested they take Ricky for lunch at the local pizza parlor the next day after they went to church.

Emily tried to hide her surprise, and agreed immediately, trying to leave His work in His hands. She woke several times in the night, sure she'd heard Ricky, only to find the little boy sound asleep.

The sermon that day was based upon a verse from the New Testament in which Paul prayed for sinners to turn away from darkness in order to receive the freedom of forgiveness and enable them to see the riches God promises for their future.

As they were leaving the sanctuary, Ricky ran to greet his friends, and Emily and Kevin made their way to the doorway where Pastor Mike was waiting. Emily reached out her hand to shake his, and was surprised when Kevin lifted her left hand to show Mike the engagement ring. Still unsure whether Kevin had made a decision about having a family, she had been hesitant to make any announcements.

Kevin's voice was deep and matter-of-fact. "We need to set up a time to visit, Mike."

Mike smiled, a knowing look of confidence on his face. "Call me this afternoon, and we'll set up an appointment." He looked at Emily and winked. "I see Ricky's here."

She hoped Kevin missed the question in Mike's remark.

"He's here for a visit. His grandparents need a break."

The pastor's smile gave her courage to hope. "I see."

When Laura and Bryan rushed up to her, she realized everyone already knew about her tentative engagement.

After Sunday school, Kevin took them home to change; then they went for lunch. Ricky was a chatterbox. It took nearly an hour for them to get him to eat. Before leaving, they let Ricky play games and ride the kiddie rides until well past his quiet time.

Once they were home again, Emily read a story to Ricky and left him to rest. "Katarina will be here with you. Kevin and I need to run some errands."

"Okay. Bye." The look of trust in his eyes was something Emily would never take for granted. His blond hair was the same color as Kevin's, and she could almost imagine he was their natural son.

Emily descended the stairs, mentally preparing herself for a difficult conversation. Katarina and Kevin were joking around together, and Emily had to interrupt. "Kat, could you keep an eye on Ricky? We need to get out for a while."

Kevin's smile softened her nervousness momentarily. As soon as they were alone in his truck, however, it started again.

"This is a pleasant surprise. I thought you'd want to stay home with Ricky this afternoon." He paused, then leaned back and started the engine. "Where are we going?"

"I don't care." She smiled, though panic was building inside her. "We need to talk."

"About what now?" He turned off Main Street, across town, and headed up the hill to his house. The clouds rolled in, making the skies dark and dreary.

"Your telling Pastor Mike that we need to set up an appointment, for one thing."

Kevin ran his hand over his chin. "Isn't that the usual step after getting engaged?"

The pickup lumbered up the curb and to a stop in his driveway as drizzle clouded the windows. Kevin shifted into Park and looked at her impatiently. He motioned toward the house. "Do you want to go inside?"

The more distance there was between them, the easier it would be to ask all the questions she'd avoided asking, and the ones he'd carefully avoided bringing to her attention, as well. She shook her head. "This is fine."

"I need to know everything, Kevin. Why you wouldn't come to Maryland with me, why you never married, why you don't want children. Why you haven't told me once that you love me."

"What brought this on?" he mumbled.

"We broke through to the next level of commitment last weekend, but there's one issue you seem to have forgotten. I want a family, and love, and you.

I've waited a long, long time, Kevin. I need to know exactly what it is that's standing in our way."

Kevin was a complex, sensitive man, and she could feel the pain his recollection of the past eight years revealed. Holding nothing back, he shared the roller coaster of family joys and sorrows all over again—his father's death, his sister having and losing her child, having to close the doors of his father's business. She respected him all the more for his honesty.

Emily was filled with guilt. All these years, she'd thought Kevin had selfishly walked away. She'd thought he'd abandoned her. She couldn't have been more wrong. Yet still, she felt betrayed. He hadn't trusted her, hadn't let her share his pain. And that confirmed he hadn't been ready for sharing good times and bad.

"You didn't even tell me your dad was sick before the engagement, Kevin!"

He looked at her, tears hiding in the corners of his eyes. "Mom and Dad asked me to wait until after we returned from our honeymoon. They didn't want anything to ruin the wedding for us."

Emily swallowed, grimacing as tears fell. "I wouldn't have left you to handle that alone."

"Why do you think I didn't tell you? I couldn't promise you a degree. I couldn't give you what Johns Hopkins could. I couldn't take your dreams away. And even now, after seeing what losing baby Lexie did to Kirk and Elizabeth, I just don't know if I can take the chance of losing a child." He reached out and took hold of her hand, pulling her across the seat.

She let out a deep sob and raised her fists, pounding softly against Kevin's solid chest as he pulled her into his embrace. "How dare you, Kevin?" She wept, not only for her own loss, but for what it had cost Kevin, as well. "How dare you?"

"Yeah, yeah." Kevin tenderly brushed the hair from her face. "I'm sorry, Em. I didn't want to take all your dreams away."

"You did cost me my dreams, you fool! All these years, we could have been together. We could have been sharing the good *and* bad, Kevin. Isn't that what you told me? Marriage is a fifty-fifty agreement?" Emily wondered if there was any hope for them to live happily ever after. If anything, they were even more independent than they had been then. "I still want those dreams, Kevin," she whispered.

Her face was tucked against Kevin's neck, and she felt him swallow. A deep sigh was followed by a ragged heave. "I wish I could give them back, Emmy. Truly I do. I thought maybe being together would be enough."

"You can, Kevin. You changed your mind about marriage...."

Emily felt him shake his head. "I don't think so."

She pulled away and looked him in the eye. "Why?"

"I thought it would be enough to have each other. I hoped I could at least be the man of your dreams in one respect. But a child is so helpless.... You deserve better."

She laughed bitterly, searching frantically for a tissue to dry her tears. "How could I ask for better than a man who selflessly put my dreams ahead of his own? Who respected his parents' needs over his own desires? Who will take time for a hurting little boy! Who is so afraid of hurting me again that he's choosing *not* to love?'' Tears blinded her and choked her voice. ''Tell me you don't love me anymore, Kevin.''

He backed away. Emily turned his jaw, forcing him to look at her. Silently she pleaded with him. As each moment of silence passed, her hope faded a little more.

''Say it—'I don't love you, Emily... I can't ever love you, Emily.' *Say it.* Once and for all, set me free, if that's what you want!''

''You're a doctor,'' he whispered. ''Surely you know how to fix a broken heart.''

Emily was filled with inadequacy. There was a long, brittle silence between them. ''God gave me a lot of knowledge, Kevin, but this wasn't in any textbook I ever read.'' She hugged him close. ''I can give you my love. I can tell you that whatever it is you think I can't deal with, *we* can. I can tell you that if you want it badly enough, God is waiting to take your pain away.''

Kevin's eyes misted, like the drizzling rain outside. Emily knew she had reached the true crux of his battle. *Please, God, give me the words to comfort him. I need him. Ricky needs him. And he needs You so badly.*

''It's just not that easy, Emmy.''

Emily reached her arm behind him, the confines of the truck making it awkward to hold him. ''Let's go outside.''

They walked to the ivy-covered gazebo in the backyard and sat down on the porch swing. Emily watched the rain fall as she coaxed Kevin to dig deeper. Finally, he admitted that he had lashed out in anger at God for allowing the doctors to give his father false hope, and for taking a tiny baby away, tearing apart his sister's marriage. ''I turned to the only comfort I could without risking losing my heart again. So you see, Em, even though I'd like to be the man you fell in love with, I can't go back.''

Emily had to admit to feeling a twinge of jealousy after Kevin's admission, yet quickly forced the negative emotion away. He wasn't giving himself credit for turning away from the temptations that had led him so far from Christ.

''Look at those leaves, Kevin. Every day wind and dirt gather on them, just like humans who can't stop sinning. Yet just as easily as that rain washes the dirt away, Christ died on the cross to free us from sin. You're no different from anyone else, in that respect. It's human nature.''

''There are always going to be reminders, Emily.''

''Only if you let there be. If God doesn't keep tally of our sins, who are *we* to keep a list? If you've handed them to God, they're gone. I don't care what happened before we met again—just so's it's only me now.''

''I couldn't bear to hurt you again, Emily.''

''I can't bear another day without you in it. You were my first and only love, Kevin. I want to marry you, to have your children, to be there on good days and bad ones.''

''Which is exactly why you deserve better than what I can give you now. Our careers barely leave time for ourselves. We've already seen that. How can we fit each other, let alone a family, into this craziness?'' Kevin stood, pushing the swing into frantic motion.

Emily stopped the swing and followed him to the

arched opening in the gazebo, where she smelled the sweet hint of lilacs already in bloom. She took hold of his arm and leaned her head on his shoulder. It was time to tell him about Ricky. About her decision to become the little boy's mother.

She couldn't allow Kevin to commit to her without understanding that she absolutely refused to give up her complete set of dreams. If he wanted her, he had to accept her—and Ricky. She felt the tears sting her eyes. It wasn't the way she had expected to become a mother, but He had given her a child nonetheless, and she wouldn't walk away from Ricky any more than she would walk away from Kevin.

Kevin turned to face Emily and buried his face in her hair. His hands moved gently to embrace her.

She had to tell him, before...

Her misgivings increased by the second. What if he said no? Could she survive his walking away again? "Kevin—"

"You're right, Emmy. I've never stopped loving you. I always will." His words were a bridge that she hoped would continue to build as he allowed God to heal his pain.

She looked into his eyes and drowned in the truth. He loved her. Always had. Always would? She blinked, feeling light-headed.

Emily forced her gaze to lock with his. "Wait. Please. Don't say anything more."

Kevin laughed. "Now that's just like a woman to change her mind. I thought this is what you wanted. You and me forever, just the way it should have been eight years ago."

Emily tore herself from his embrace. "Listen to me. I'm going to be a mother."

A sudden icy contempt flashed in his eyes.

"A what?"

"I'm going to have a child. A son, actually."

"All this talk of a future, of love, of acceptance, and lies and repentance, and you somehow managed to forget to mention you're pregnant?"

She reached for him, and he backed away. "It's not what you think."

Emily was going to be a mother?

Kevin felt his chest tighten. *A baby.* He dragged in a deep breath, choking on the heavy scent of spring. Flowers and rain, and love. He looked for an escape from this cage.

"How—" His voice caught. He didn't really want to know any more. Didn't want to have to walk away. Didn't want to see the pain in Emily's green eyes when he broke her heart again. His voice caught, as he tried to recall the information she'd told him. His eyes roamed over her slender figure.

She placed a hand on her stomach and shook her head. "It's Ricky."

"Whoa, Em. You said his parents died—" he paused to think "—and that he was only visiting."

Emily nodded, her red hair bouncing with the slight movement. "His grandparents can't care for him full-time. They didn't want him in limbo any longer. I tried to put it off, but inside I knew they were right. It was time to decide—either I adopt him, or find him another family who could give him a permanent home." She paused. "When I got there to pick him up, I knew."

"And why didn't you tell me sooner?"

"Because my love for Ricky will matter in his life. It isn't something I can turn away from any more than if I'd carried him in my own womb. I can't explain it, Kevin. I just know that God brought Ricky to me for a reason.'' She spoke with bitterness. ''I guess I kept hoping you would tell me you were ready to make all of *our* dreams come true. You, me, happily ever after, kids, dogs—all of those things that turn a house into a home. I want it all, Kevin. For once in my life, I thought there was a chance to—'' Emily's voice broke, and he felt a knot in his own throat, as well. ''If you remember, you were the one who wanted a house full of children.''

He couldn't look at her. ''I was young and idealistic.''

There was a long painful silence, and Emily turned, tipping her head up as if to question God Himself. ''I guess we both were, then, because I believed in those dreams. And I'm tired of waiting for someone else to make them come true.'' Her voice was edged with confidence and determination. ''I guess the only other question I have for you is, Will the man of my dreams be able to make the rest of my dreams come true?''

Chapter Eighteen

Kevin struggled to understand how Emily could have made such a decision alone. Yes, he wanted them to be together—but kids? They'd overcome one hurdle; surely they would eventually have come to some sort of agreement about children, too.

He rubbed his temples. *What a lousy day!* He didn't want to accept that the doctors were right about having to take it slow in returning to work. Kevin dropped onto the sofa and spread the full length, propping his head on that all-too-familiar pillow.

Alex came into the room. "You feeling okay?"

"Growing up is the pits, Alex. I thought I could stay twenty-two forever, just live it over and over. You know?"

His brother sat down in the recliner. "I'm sorry, Kev. I thought we did the right thing at the time. Maybe not."

"I'm not talking about Dad's business, Alex. I'm happier running my own company than I ever was having to worry about whether Dad would have done it the same way, or whether a job would bring in enough to pay the employees and leave enough money for Mom, too. I should've told you that long ago. It hurt at the time, but we did the right thing."

"If that's not it, what is it?"

Kevin chuckled. "Life, love, the pursuit of those pesky dreams."

"I saw Emily walking off. She okay?" He paused. "Doesn't she realize it's raining?"

"She insisted on walking home." Kevin leaned his head back, wishing this headache would subside. "She just became a mother."

"She what?"

"She's going to adopt Ricky—the little boy whose parents died. They named her as guardian, and she just decided today to adopt him."

Alex let out a whistle. "That woman has spunk."

Kevin couldn't argue with that. In her quiet conservative way, she had overcome a lifetime of obstacles. He, on the other hand, had life pretty easy in comparison, had taken it for granted, and was doing a lousy job rebuilding it after the few catastrophes he'd experienced.

"You know, Kevin, I think you need to get away and spend some time talking to God. Get your priorities straight before you lose Emily again."

"That's like the pot calling the kettle black. You never married. Why?"

"Never found a lady who could commit to a man who jumped into forest fires for a living."

Kevin nodded. "Then why do you keep doing it?"

"Hey there, bro, this is your analysis, not mine."

"Not yet, anyway." Kevin closed his eyes, hoping his brother would take the hint and leave him alone.

"Why are you afraid to be a father, Kevin?"

Alex never was one to take a hint.

Kevin took a deep breath and exhaled. "After seeing all of us suffer after Dad died, then Elizabeth and Kirk's marriage fall apart when baby Lexie died, it seemed a whole lot easier to avoid the issue all the way around."

Kevin heard a soft agreement from across the room and looked up at his brother.

Nodding, Alex added, "Same reason I spent eight years jumping into fires. We're all going to die, and I suspect it isn't nearly as frightening to go as it is to be left behind. But, Kevin, losing Emily a second time would be twice as rough as it was the first time. You know that, don't you?"

He nodded, remembering the day he and Ricky had built the playhouse, and the evening they'd watched the Beaumont kids, and all those months Jacob and Bryan had lived with him. He loved kids, he couldn't deny it. But becoming a father was such a huge commitment. And his business alone was enough to keep him busy at this point in time. How would he ever make time for being a husband *and* father?

"And what's standing in your way?"

Kevin thought. Was it really his past that he couldn't deal with, or was that merely an excuse? Was it Emily's dreams, or Ricky? "You know, when I was twenty, being a dad and a husband and keeping a job didn't seem like it would be any problem. But now...I can't even handle my job."

"You can't beat yourself up over that. You need

some time, then you'll be right back on top of things.''

That wasn't what he'd meant. Since his accident, he had felt unsettled. Edgy. Out of control. Everything he'd worked for was in jeopardy. He couldn't even accept Emily's love and forgiveness. He'd been offered a priceless gift; unworthy as he was, Emily had offered it to him. Her love. Acceptance. Support.

''You know, Kevin, a friend out in the field told me one day that it wasn't as important to know who you are, as *whose* you are. Once you have that straight, all the rest falls into place.''

''I can tell you from experience, that's a whole lot easier than it sounds.''

''We're all lost sheep, Kevin. Not one of us is worthy of His grace.'' Alex shook his head and took a drink of his soda. ''I know what you've been going through these last few years. I've had my share of arguments with God, too. But here's a reason you didn't die. Take some time off. Get some rest. Open your eyes, before it's too late.''

Alex went upstairs to the den. Kevin heard his brother thumbing through papers on his desk.

A week later, Kevin called Alex at the clinic and told him he was taking a few days off. ''You're right, I'm no good to anyone like this.''

''It's not all that bad, bro. Looking at what-all you've accomplished with your business in a mere six years, it's obvious you haven't had a life outside the company. You need someone to share your load here, permanently. We would make a great team,'' Alex said.

Kevin shook his head. ''I know we would. I've

been meaning to discuss that with you. First things first, and sorry, but my business isn't it. I need you to hold things together."

"Not a problem. I'm here for you." They reviewed the building schedule. Alex had come in and taken over the supervisory position on the site with poise, gaining the respect of the entire crew by asking what he didn't already know about the job. For the first time in six years, Kevin felt at ease taking a week off. "Alex, I am thinking seriously about your suggestion. I can't thank you enough for helping me out. By the way, the crew's paychecks are on my desk in the den. Yours is there, too."

"Thanks. You take whatever time you need. We're going to finish this project on time."

Kevin left him the phone number at Laura and Bryan's cabin. The couple had decided to add on to the bungalow to accommodate their growing family. He couldn't blame them. It was a great place to get away from the pressures of the city.

He hoped that a few days up there would put his problems back in perspective. He'd do a little work, fish for a while, have a talk or two with God; get his priorities straight.

Just what the doctor ordered. He laughed at his own bad joke. It had been a week since Emily had dropped the latest bomb on his life.

Kids. She wanted not only one, but several. She didn't just want love, she wanted the complete dream, as she'd reminded him in a phone conversation the previous day. She wanted him despite his past. Wanted to share his life, his burdens, his business, fifty-fifty. Kids, dogs and all the upgrades, as she put it.

He pulled into the dirt driveway and opened the gate, then closed it behind him before continuing to the back side of the cabin. He unloaded his duffel bag, the fishing pole, then the groceries: a sack of man-size frozen dinners, a few assorted snacks, plus two gallons of milk. He filled the refrigerator and plugged it in.

The June sun was high in the sky, warming the cabin through the big plate-glass window. Despite its warmth, Kevin brought in an armful of kindling, dropped it in the copper boiler and went back outside. He dug through the shed out back 'til he found the sledgehammer and splitting wedge. He and Bryan usually tried to save the split wood in the wood box for the dead of winter when it was too cold and blustery. Which left out today. Spring had made an early arrival in the Rockies.

What little snow had fallen the past winter had melted, and the ice was gone from the river below. He tossed a few logs away from the sod-covered garage. He propped a log on the old tree stump, tapped the wedge into the wood and swung the sledge. The broken pieces fell to the ground.

It felt good to exert some energy. The ache in his muscles sure beat the ache in his heart. He repeated the motions several times, then carried the wood inside and built a fire as the sun set.

Kevin had spent the past week thinking about little besides Emily and Ricky. He popped a frozen dinner into the microwave and moved the chair so he could watch the sunset. He went to bed early, thankful for the full bin of firewood that had exhausted him so he could sleep.

First thing the next morning, Kevin strung his fly

pole and headed to the river. A couple of hours later, he headed back, his stringer loaded with half a dozen twelve-inch rainbow trout. He cleaned the fish, then planned to get busy drafting the layout of the cabin so he could give Laura and Bryan his suggestions for remodeling.

He and Bryan had agreed that a new fence around the cabin, in order to keep the kids away from the river, was the first project they would tackle. The next question was whether they wanted to add on a traditional frame structure, or hire a log-home contractor to try to match the original cabin. Kevin had agreed to start with his suggestions, then let them consider the other as an option.

He walked through the gap in the pole-fence and onto the Beaumont property, just in time to hear car doors slam at the front of the cabin. Female voices carried through the trees.

"Who in the world could be here?"

Kevin climbed the steps to the veranda and propped his pole against the corner joint of the logs, then walked in the back door of the cabin.

Ricky's bright blue eyes greeted him. "Kevin!"

Emily followed, her arms overloaded with luggage. "Kevin?"

Next were Emily's sisters and her mother.

Kevin staggered back, feeling as if he'd just been ambushed. "Hi. I didn't realize you were coming."

Emily looked at him, and the room grew silent except for the sound of Ricky's feet running on the bare oak floors.

"Let me get some of that for you." He reached for the luggage, and accidentally slung the stringer of trout at one of the bags. "Oh, sorry."

Lisa and Katarina jumped back, screeching. Ricky ran back down from the bedroom to see what had happened. Kevin took the fish to the kitchen sink and rinsed his hands, then returned.

"Are you going to take me fishing, Kevin?"

Kevin looked at Ricky, then Emily, waiting for her to answer. When she didn't, he said, "I don't know, sport. I didn't know anyone was coming up here this week, so I should probably get out of your hair."

Ricky scratched his head. "He's not in our hair, is he, Emily?"

"I'm sure Kevin doesn't want to stay here with a cabin full of women," Emily's mother snipped.

Emily grinned, pursing her lips to keep from laughing aloud at the irony of her mother's remark. She could think of no more comfortable place for Kevin than a room full of women, unless one of those women was her mother. She looked to Kevin for understanding, sending a silent apology.

"Someone forgot to mention you were scheduled to use the cabin for this week. I came up to see what they're going to need to do to make room for the whole family. I'll have my things packed up in just a few minutes." Kevin turned toward the kitchen.

Katarina looped her hand through Kevin's, stopping him. She addressed her sister. "What a perfect time to celebrate the engagement, isn't it, Lisa? You have to stay, Kevin."

The youngest of the sisters gazed at her mother, then at Emily. "Of course it is. Congratulations, Kevin. Ricky, why don't we go outside and get your things from the van."

It was Kevin's turn to look to Emily for an explanation.

Emily's mother, Naomi, turned her back. "I won't believe it until I see it. He left you once, Emily. There's nothing to stop him from doing it again."

"Mother, I love Kevin more than ever. I'm not asking for your approval. If you want to let your bitterness ruin your life, that's up to you. I'd rather forgive than live in the chains of unhappiness."

"You can't be serious, Emily. You're telling me that you've forgiven even your father? How can you forgive a father abandoning his wife and children?"

Emily swallowed hard. "Oh, Mom." Emily wrapped her arms around her mother. "I don't ever deny the pain. I just don't let it control me any longer. I've handed it to God." Her mother started to complain about her husband again, and Emily interrupted. "I don't want or need to hear it anymore. I've put that behind me. There's no reason to rehash something I have no control over."

Naomi looked at Kevin, then back to Emily. "Don't expect me to help with another wedding."

"I didn't plan on it, but if you'd like to come, you'd be welcome." Naomi stomped out the door, and Emily's shoulders drooped.

Kevin wrapped his arms around her and kissed her forehead. "I don't want to ruin your mother's visit, Emily."

"If you want to stay, stay, Kevin. Your leaving won't improve her attitude."

"What do you want?" He took her left hand in his, touching the ring he'd given her. Dare he believe there was a chance it would remain on her finger forever this time?

"I want you here. You know that. Question is, do you want to stay?"

Chapter Nineteen

Emily was grateful that Kevin agreed to stay. Her sisters offered their continued support for her and Kevin, each taking a turn talking to Naomi. Emily doubted there was any hope of her mother changing her attitude after all these years. Though Emily longed for her mother to be happy for her just once in her life, she no longer depended upon it.

She and Ricky "helped" Kevin take measurements of the cabin for Kevin's drafting, while Katarina and Lisa took Naomi to Estes Park to shop. When they were finished, Kevin fixed a pitcher of lemonade and poured three glasses. He and Emily sat on the veranda, while Ricky gathered pinecones.

"I'm sorry I put you on the spot this morning, Kevin."

He took a long drink, then rested the glass on his knee. "I noticed a load of bricks falling, but for the life of me, I couldn't figure a way to dodge it." He turned to her and his whole face spread into a smile.

She took his hand, grateful he could laugh about it already.

Kevin tipped the chair back and stretched. "I must admit, under the circumstances I'm surprised you're still wearing the ring. I half expected it to come off immediately when I couldn't commit, and definitely thought you'd take it off when your mother arrived."

Guessing that meant he hadn't come to any decision yet, Emily said simply, "It gives me hope."

Kevin leaned over the side of the chair and pressed his lips against hers, and Emily fought the temptation to assume everything was going to turn out the way she wanted it to. She was too old to presume that. Despite her fears, though, she wouldn't give up hope. *God is still in the miracle business.*

"Mommy? I mean Emily..." The soft words were accompanied by a gentle tap on her knee.

Emily jumped and looked around. She looked back to Kevin, tears instantly forming. "Yes, Ricky?" Even though it was a mistake, it tugged on her emotions and gave her hope that one day he would accept her as his mother.

She rested her hand on his shoulder. "What, Ricky?"

"Can we go see the water?"

"Sure. We can take a walk to the river. Ask Kevin if he wants to come with us. Maybe he'd even show us how he caught all those trout for supper." She smiled at Kevin, daring him to turn the charming little boy down.

Kevin waited casually, pretending he hadn't heard a word Emily had said. *Please, help Kevin to see how much he would love being a daddy, God. And help me to give him the time he needs to decide.* She looked up, thrilled to see Kevin put Ricky on his shoulders and grab the fishing pole.

They spent the afternoon fishing and hiking along the banks, gathering sticks and pinecones. The flowers were just beginning to bloom, and Ricky wanted to pick all of them.

"If you leave them for a few more days, they'll be much prettier," Emily suggested. "Then we can pick two or three, but not all of them." He scrunched up his face at the advice, but settled instead for making a pouch from his T-shirt to hold the collectibles he found along the path. When they returned to the cabin, Emily helped him make a centerpiece from the twigs and clusters of cones and various other "treasures."

While Kevin prepared the fish, Emily put a bowl of broccoli in the microwave and buttered a loaf of French bread. Her mother and sisters returned while dinner was cooking. After they all ate, Emily bathed Ricky and put him to bed upstairs on a folding cot.

Kevin was increasingly disappointed that he hadn't spent much time alone. There was nowhere to escape, and he was impatient to get started on the cabin. He knew Bryan was, too. Kevin couldn't imagine what four kids sounded like within these walls. Ricky seemed to echo off them all by himself.

Emily brought some needlework with her, and filled any spare time with that. Naomi had her knitting, Katarina brought books, and Lisa had her paints and easel. Her project for this week was a portrait of Emily and her new son. Kevin loved watching her work, especially when the subject was so interesting.

Once they were satisfied that Ricky was asleep, Emily suggested a moonlight walk. They both welcomed the break from the stress inside.

"Mom seems to be adjusting to everything. She's thrilled to have a grandchild, finally," she said as they strolled.

Kevin laughed. "How did she expect to get grandkids when she did her best to chase any husband-prospects away?"

Emily didn't say anything, but snuggled closer. Even he was chilled by the cool evening air. "I guess I'm a fine one to talk, aren't I? It's not that I don't like kids, Emily. It's not even that I don't want them. You know I always wanted us to have a house full of little ones."

"I remember," she said softly. "I'm not trying to pressure you, Kevin. I just need you to know where I'm at. If you decide you can't commit to me and Ricky…I'll manage, and so will you."

He leaned his head against hers. "I feel like some ogre. We were younger then. Young and naive. Taking a chance at hurting you again is bad enough, but to think of involving kids…like Ricky. He's already lost his mother and father. What if I had died after that accident?"

"You didn't die, Kevin. It was a freak accident. If you hadn't choked on that candy, we wouldn't have made nearly the issue over it."

He shrugged. "It's not just that. We weren't absorbed in careers eight years ago. I don't know how I can back off now that business is booming, Emmy."

She knew what he was feeling and understood his

doubts. There were no easy answers. "Kevin, don't worry. I'm not going anywhere. You don't have to give me an answer today."

Kevin stopped walking and pulled her into his embrace. "I think Alex was right."

"About what?" Emily asked, wrapping her arms around him.

"I need my head examined for having even one doubt, don't I?"

Kevin pulled a sleeping bag and pillow from the closet and moved out to the veranda to sleep. The stars were bright and the mountain air was crisp. Even when he snuggled to the bottom of the bag, his shoulders stuck out.

He went back inside to grab a sweatshirt from his bag and was surprised to hear the sisters still giggling as if they were having a slumber party. He slipped back outside unnoticed, wondering how Ricky could sleep through the noise. The little tike was his last thought upon falling asleep, and his first upon waking up.

Ricky greeted him early the next morning, completely dressed, well before anyone was awake inside. Kevin left a note on the table and took Ricky fishing. They made a short pole from a willow branch and fishing line, and sat on a grassy spot along the bank, next to a quiet spot in the river.

The little boy's cough started with an occasional ticklish sound. Kevin didn't think much of it, but after a while it became more constant. "You catching a cold, Ricky?"

"No, just a cough. I have medicine to take. Dr. Em—Emily gives it to me."

"Let's head back and see what Emily has planned for breakfast, shall we?"

Ricky eagerly pulled in his empty line and ran up the hill to the cabin, with Kevin puffing and panting close behind.

Kevin got Ricky a glass of juice and told Emily about the cough. After listening to Ricky's chest, she gave him his asthma medicine. By midmorning, Ricky was feeling better, his cough was much quieter, and he went from one activity to another at lightning speed. Kevin worked outside until lunch, trying not to intrude on the women's time together.

Before long, Ricky made his way outside, too. "Kevin, will you play football with me?"

Kevin reached his hands out, expecting a little toss. Ricky wound up and slammed him in the chest with the sponge ball. "Nice throw." He stepped farther back and returned the ball. They continued playing until Emily called them for lunch.

The tension among all of them eased as the week went on, so much so that Naomi eventually offered to watch Ricky so Kevin and Emily could get away for an afternoon.

Emily didn't hesitate for a moment. On the way out the door, she grabbed the pole in one hand and took his hand in the other. "I want to fish. Will you teach me?"

"We've been fishing all week. Why haven't you asked earlier?"

She shrugged. "I was busy keeping an eye on

Ricky. Since he's napping now and Naomi's babysitting, I can relax and enjoy it."

They hiked farther downstream to an area with fewer trees to get caught on, then set down the tackle box. Kevin tied a fly and showed her how to "strip" the line. Then, standing behind her, he held her arm, showing her the rhythm of casting the line back and forth, letting out more line with each cast.

Emily began to get the idea, so Kevin let her go on her own. He whispered suggestions as if it were some sort of secret. She turned her head to talk to him, and the line went wild. She cast forward, and her arm jerked to a sudden end.

"Oh, no, I'm caught on something."

Kevin felt a tug on his shirt and laughed. "Looks like a big one." He twisted around to try to grab the hook from his back, then saw the line arc from him to the willows at their right, then over to Emily. Kevin walked over, hoping to untangle it without losing the fly. Emily turned. Kevin ducked under the pole, and the line snapped loose. The hook tugged his shirt again, and Kevin swung his arms, trying to avoid the line getting tangled around him.

"Emily! Kevin!" Lisa called. "Ke-e-e-vin! E-em-m-m-ily!

Kevin turned just as Emily did, and the two wound up fighting each other's efforts. "Lisa, we're down here."

"Hurry up here. Something's wrong with Ricky!"

Emily started up the hill, and was quickly jerked backwards. "Kevin!"

"I'm trying to reach my knife, just a minute. The hook is caught in my shirt." Emily turned to look, and whacked Kevin in the head with the pole. "Stop tugging, Emily, you're making it worse. And drop the pole, would you?" Once he was able to get his hand into his pocket, he cut the line, and they both bolted up the hill.

Emily ran into the cabin, directly toward the horrible wheezing sound. "Get his medicine."

Katarina handed it to Emily, adding, "We just gave him two puffs a few minutes ago."

"Let's get him to the hospital. Call ahead for us."

Kevin carried Ricky outside, then tried to hand him to Emily, but the little boy tightened his grip around Kevin's neck while continuing to gasp for air. "I guess you're driving, Em. I'll sit in back with him."

He turned to the preschooler. "Watch, Ricky. I'm going to buckle my seat belt right here next to you. But I need you to sit in your seat, so we're both safe. Okay?" Before Kevin detached the boy's arms from around his neck, he buckled his seat belt across his lap and showed Ricky. "It's your turn now."

Kevin couldn't believe the drastic change in Ricky's condition in such a short time. It was a struggle for him to breathe.

"See if you can get him to take another puff from the inhaler. I don't think he's breathing deeply enough to help much, but we're going to have to keep trying. As soon as we get him to the hospital, they'll set up the nebulizer treatment."

Kevin shook the medicine, then held the mask over Ricky's nose and mouth. "Come on, sport, I need you to take a really deep breath." Kevin gently coaxed him to keep inhaling. He brushed the damp hair from Ricky's brow and wiped the perspiration with his shirtsleeve. Just as Ricky tried to inhale, he went into another coughing spasm. By the time they reached the hospital twenty minutes later, the wheezing had deteriorated to a high-pitched whistle, and Ricky seemed too weak to care who was holding him.

Emily pulled into the emergency room parking lot. "I'm going to go order the medicine and get him admitted, while you bring him in."

"You're so good at giving orders," he teased, giving her a wink of encouragement.

She put the car in Park and ran inside.

"Ricky, we're going into the hospital to get you help."

"Daddy?"

Kevin stopped dead in his tracks. "It's me, Kevin."

"My new daddy," the boy said slowly. He smiled and put his head on Kevin's shoulder. "Emmy, my new mommy." Just saying those few words seemed to exhaust him.

Kevin felt love seep through him. He was unconditionally loved by a little boy who had lost everyone dear to him, everyone except his new mommy. A little boy who had every reason to be angry, yet trusted God, trusted Emily, trusted him. Just because. There were no strings, no conditions, just love.

It was enough. Just love... *Okay, God, I get the message, loud and clear. If I could ask a favor, it's that You let me have a chance to be Ricky's daddy.*

Kevin closed the car and was inside before he realized it. When Ricky saw the doors to the emergency room, his body grew tense, and Kevin held him closer than ever.

"I know how you feel, Ricky. I don't like this place, either, but they're going to help you. Just take it easy. I'll stay right here with you."

I'm not about to let you go. All the way down the corridor Kevin found himself breathing more deeply, as if doing so would benefit Ricky.

He suddenly realized that Ricky would be alone if it weren't for Emily. Of course, somebody would see that his essential needs were met, but it wouldn't be the same.

He recognized the love in Emily's gaze when she looked at Ricky; it was the same tender gaze she gave Kevin.

Suddenly it was no longer a matter of Ricky needing Kevin, but of Kevin needing Ricky—the little boy who had the wisdom to teach Kevin all about what was important in life.

Love.

Not money. Not jobs. Not business commitments.

Just *love.*

Emily met him at the door and led Kevin to the nurse who was waiting with the treatment, then paused. "I need to finish filling out the forms."

"You go ahead, Em. I'll take care of Ricky." He sat down and turned Ricky in his lap so the nebulizer pipe could blow directly on Ricky's face. With each gasp for air, Ricky's laboring lessened slightly.

"We'll need to take his vitals and listen to his lungs, Mr. Berthoff, if you could please undress your son."

Kevin laughed to himself, suddenly flattered to be

mistaken not only for a married man, but for a father. He must be doing okay at the job if he'd already convinced one nurse. The moment of humor was a welcome reprieve. "Come on, Ricky. Let's show the nurse your muscles."

She took over holding the pipe, while Kevin undressed Ricky. Kevin tugged on the sleeves of the boy's gold-and-black CU Buffs football sweatshirt and gently worked it over his blond head. The toddler squirmed in Kevin's lap, snuggling closer as if cold. Kevin indulged in the chance to wrap his arms around the boy to keep him warm.

After the treatment, the nurse put an oxygen mask over Ricky's mouth and nose. A doctor arrived and wrapped his hand around the metal disk of the stethoscope to warm it for a minute, then placed it against Ricky's back.

It was as if Kevin were back in the hospital himself, watching as the doctor listened to the little boy's lungs and heart. Kevin looked up, surprised to see Emily standing calmly in the doorway with her gaze fixed on him.

In that moment, he realized that God had given him another chance to have the love and happiness he had pushed so far away. He had allowed Emily's love to heal him. Kevin winked, and gave her a slow, secret smile, which he knew she understood.

They were a family.

Emily stepped closer and knelt next to the chair. "How's he doing?"

"Better. Aren't you, sport."

Ricky nodded.

"Thank you for coming along, Kevin."

"That's part of being a dad, isn't it?" He smiled.

Emily's mouth gaped open. As soon as they were alone, she looked at him with hope in her eyes. "Are you serious?"

"Of course I'm serious. I'd never joke about becoming a father."

The nurse returned a while later. "Mr. Berthoff, Dr. Berthoff, this is a prescription for Ricky's medicine..."

Emily looked at Kevin and started to correct the nurse, but Kevin shook his head and winked. *What in the world are you up to, Kevin MacIntyre?*

"If you'll just sign here, you can take your son home. The doctor is comfortable with you monitoring his treatments." The nurse gave Emily more instructions and handed her a form to sign, while Kevin dressed Ricky.

On the way out the door, Emily looked up at the two blond men in her life. "'Mr. Berthoff'?" she repeated incredulously. "Isn't that carrying your point a bit far?"

He chuckled. "I thought it was kind of cute, myself. And I will say, I definitely liked being mistaken for your husband." He paused. "Ricky, what do you think of adopting a mommy and a daddy?"

"Yeah! Can I have a brother and a sister, too?"

Kevin laughed. "We'll have to wait and see what God has planned on that one." He looked at Emily. "I know it's been like beating your head against a wall, Emily, but this little guy here finally drove the point home. What do you think of becoming Mrs.-Dr.-Emily-Berthoff-MacIntyre? Or whatever you want to be called."

"I think...it's about time." Emily smiled and leaned forward to give Ricky, then Kevin, a kiss.

"Are you twitterpated *now,* Dr. Em—Mom?" Ricky asked, his voice raspy.

"Yes, Ricky, I am." She looked at Kevin again. "Always was," she murmured.

"Don't I know it! We'd better get back to the cabin. Your mom and sisters are going to wonder what happened to us."

Chapter Twenty

First thing Monday morning, Emily arranged to take a few weeks of family leave. She and Kevin took Ricky to see a specialist so they could learn more about controlling his asthma. As far as they could tell, his attack in the mountains had been caused by the high levels of pollen and dust. Now he was improving.

Emily was scheduled to sign the adoption papers that Wednesday, but postponed it so she and Kevin both could do so after the wedding ceremony.

With all the changes Ricky had already been through, she and Kevin had decided it would be easier on everyone if there wasn't a long engagement. That way, when Emily went back to work, their family would already have settled into their own routine, however chaotic.

She called George and Harriet and put Ricky on the phone. "I'm going to get a new mommy *and* a new daddy. Dr. Emmy is getting married to Kevin this Saturday." Emily laughed at how quickly Ricky was picking up new expressions from Kevin, such as calling her Emmy. The two were inseparable, just as a father and son should be, she thought.

Though this was the busiest time of the year for weddings, Pastor Mike had worked to fit them into the church schedule. She and Kevin agreed to have the ceremony in the courtyard, and have the reception at a nearby restaurant.

Her sisters and mother were troopers, pulling everything together for the small ceremony. Emily took the box out of her closet and tried her wedding dress on for the first time in eight years. Once she had it cleaned, it would be perfect.

Kevin came in after work and looked around at the piles of fabric and ribbon. "I thought this was going to be a simple ceremony—me in jeans, you in...oh, never mind, that's later. Sorry, got the ceremonies mixed up." He winked, pleased to see her cheeks turn a brilliant shade of pink. He lifted the corner of material and took a peek. "Have you seen Ricky under all this stuff recently?"

"He's playing at Laura's. They're going to bring him home after supper. By the way, what are you fixing?"

"Fixing? For dinner? Me? How about my specialty, pizza?"

Emily laughed. "Good idea. Mom doesn't like mushrooms, but anything else goes."

He looked at Naomi and smiled. "We have one thing in common, anyway."

Emily's mother smiled back. "It looks like I owe you an apology, Kevin. I should have put my own selfishness aside and let my daughters find happiness years ago."

Kevin wrapped an arm around her. "I'm in no position to criticize. I am glad you're putting the past behind you, for your own sake, as well as Emily's. And I want to thank you for giving me such a precious gift."

Naomi looked at Emily, confused. "You haven't opened my gift yet, have you?"

Emily shook her head, and Kevin chuckled mischievously. "I'm talking about Emmy. Your daughter is an incredible woman. Thank you. I promise to take good care of her and to be faithful 'til the day I die."

"I have no doubts you will, Kevin."

The doorbell rang, but Ricky didn't wait for an answer. He ran inside, dragging the Beaumont family with him. "See, Chad, I get a new daddy, too. Kevin's going to be *my* dad."

"So what, I get *two* babies!"

"I can have two, too," Ricky argued.

Laura and Bryan trailed in behind the rest of the gang. "Guess our news is history, huh?"

Emily looked at Laura, her eyes open wide. "Twins? I was wondering..."

The couple laughed. "The ultrasound you suggested was scheduled for this morning. No wonder I'm getting so big."

Kevin patted his friend's shoulder in congratulation. "Six kids? Wow."

Saturday morning was warm and sunny, a perfect day for a wedding. The organist played, and Kevin and Bryan tossed the football across the tiny church parlor as they waited for Pastor Mike to come for them. Finally the oak door opened, and Mike gave

Kevin a wide smile. "That bride of yours is beautiful, you know."

"About that visit we had in the hospital, Mike..."

"It's okay, Emily had already told me about your relationship."

Kevin put a hand on Mike's shoulder. "I was going to remind you that I meant every word of it. I love her, and I'm not going to let her go this time."

Mike laughed. "And I'm going to hold you to it! I think she's ready, what about you?"

"Ready. This is the best day of my life." Kevin turned from Mike to Bryan. "Now don't forget to give me the ring, would you?"

"Turnabout's fair play," Bryan said as he followed Mike and Kevin to the church courtyard.

"Why's that?" Kevin murmured from the corner of his mouth.

"You set Laura and me up." Bryan turned to look at him. "But I don't think either of us could have taken Laura's matchmaking much longer!"

"Remind me to thank her." Kevin smiled and heard Bryan's soft chuckle.

The organist played more loudly, then eased in to the processional, and Emily appeared at the end of the grassy aisle.

Kevin had never seen her more beautiful. The ivory dress flowed over her curves, simple yet elegant, perfectly Emily. Kevin's smile grew wider and his heart beat faster. *Thank you, Father. I don't know what took me so long to get here, but I'm sure glad You didn't give up on me.*

Naomi walked Emily down the aisle and offered her daughter's hand to Kevin. They shared a special smile, and Naomi gave him a hug.

Kevin looked into the eyes of his bride. His heart skipped a beat. The sprinkling of freckles across her nose was as charming as on the day they had first met. Flowers circled the bun on top of her head and delicate strands of her beautiful red hair framed her face.

Kevin took her hand in his. It was small and delicate, warm and reassuring. Today he was marrying his best friend, the bride of his youth, the only woman he'd ever truly loved.

"In Ecclesiastes, King Solomon tells us that two are better than one, for if one falls down, his friend can help him up...." Pastor Mike's voice faded, and Kevin realized the truth of His words.

"... Though one can be overpowered, two can defend themselves. A cord of three strands is not quickly broken. Emily and Kevin, your relationship has proven the strength of the bonds of love and forgiveness can survive the tests of time."

Emily's eyes sparkled with tears, and Kevin lifted his hand to dry them. *I love you,* he mouthed silently, as they turned to face the altar.

I love you, she mouthed in return, a look of admiration filling her gaze. Standing hand-in-hand, they bowed their heads.

Kevin heard Ricky's voice among the congregation, and knew that His timing was perfect, and that the rough eight years he and Emily had survived hadn't been wasted. He was finally ready to be a husband and a father.

"Do you, Kevin James, take Emily Ann..."

Kevin said his vows, which were echoed by Emily's softer, gentler voice, then placed the ring on Emily's finger. Surprised to find her trembling, he winked. She smiled confidently and slid the gold band on his finger.

Pastor Mike smiled. "I now pronounce you man and wife. What God has joined together, may no man put asunder." He turned to Kevin. "You may kiss the bride."

As Kevin and Emily sealed their vow with a kiss, the wedding march began.

From the corner of her eye, Emily could see Ricky squirming in his seat next to her mother. Kevin's family had all made it just in time for the ceremony.

She looked at Kevin, overwhelmed by the reflection of her love in her husband's blue eyes. She'd waited a lifetime for this day—to marry the man of her dreams. Never, though, had she imagined a day so perfect. She was not only marrying her only love and officially becoming Ricky's mother, but, most wonderful of all, she had her own mother's blessing.

"I now present Kevin and Emily MacIntyre—" Ricky ran up the aisle and into Kevin's waiting arms "—and their soon-to-be son, Ricky."

"That's my *new* mommy and daddy, Mike. They're twitterpated."

"That's my boy!" Kevin's laughter was joined by a chorus of background accompaniment.

Following the ceremony, the adoption papers were signed. Then Kevin lifted Ricky into the crook of one arm, embraced Emily with his other, and the three became a family.

When they left the church, she could see Bryan and Alex had taken it upon themselves to make certain that Kevin's truck was appropriately adorned for the festivities. Brushing the crepe paper and pop cans aside, Kevin lifted Emily and Ricky into the cab for the ride to the reception.

Her sisters and mother had left early that morning to complete the decorating. The reception area was stunning. On each ivory table were small clusters of wildflowers. And Laura had insisted on making the cake—three oval tiers of ivory with fresh wildflowers between cakes.

Among the guests were Kevin's employees and Emily's co-workers. The receiving line was one long "I told you so" followed by "playing hard-to-get, my foot!" and many hugs of joy.

"These last few weeks on the clinic are going to be interesting, aren't they?" Kevin said as he followed Emily to find his brother and twin sisters, who had arrived just before the ceremony.

Emily turned her head and smiled mischievously. "If you had just let me give you that tetanus shot without making such a scene, they wouldn't be having nearly so much fun with this."

He wrapped his arms around his wife's waist and smiled. "Then again, neither would I."

He savored the sound of Emily's deep laugh and the vanilla scent of her perfume. His willpower was wearing thin.

Kevin and Emily visited with relatives for a while before cutting the cake. Ricky and his friends were there immediately, ready for the first bite, having already eaten half a plate of the homemade butter mints.

Emily gracefully cut a bite of cake and lifted it to Kevin's mouth.

"Can we leave now?" he whispered.

"Not until you give me a bite."

"Oh, yeah, I forgot. I'd hate for you to get light-headed—yet."

Going against tradition, they served the cake themselves, enjoying another chance to visit with each of their guests.

Then they changed from their wedding clothes and rushed out the door, but the truck was gone.

"Uncle Alex moved it. I got to ride with him," Ricky exclaimed. Birdseed pelted them as they hugged Ricky goodbye.

Emily was torn over leaving him already. "Aunt Katarina will take good care of you. We'll be home in two days."

"I know," he said confidently. "Uncle Alex says he'll take me for pizza."

Emily prepared to toss the bouquet, and smiled at Kevin. "You go find a car, while I find our next bride."

Emily turned her back to the gathering of women. Just as she let the bouquet go, Kevin's clean truck pulled to a stop in front of them.

The bouquet flew high into the tree and caught in the branches. Kevin jumped up and grabbed the limb to loosen it, and it bounced off another branch and into Alex's hands.

"Oh, no, you don't." Alex batted it away, directly to Katarina.

"You two had better give in now," Kevin exclaimed as he helped Emily into her seat.

An hour later, they arrived at the hotel, and Kevin carried Emily over the threshold. "We finally made it, Doc."

"Kevin, don't you dare refer to me as your 'doctor' again, because the minute you touch me, I don't think or feel a bit doctorly. I only want to be Mrs. MacIntyre, a woman in love."

"Excuse me." Kevin stopped. "But to me, you'll always be the heart specialist. Not only did you save my life, but you fixed my broken heart, too."

"I don't know—you're the one who gave mine a jump start, remember?"

He laughed. "That kid…"

"I miss him already." She looked into his eyes. "Think he misses us?"

"With the brood at Laura and Bryan's, and his Aunt Kat and Uncle Alex to entertain him? He's probably going to be lonely once we get him home. Maybe we ought to get busy filling that house of yours—ours. After all, we were supposed to be the first ones down the aisle. We've got some catching up to do."

"We are *not* competing with the Beaumonts, Kevin."

"Maybe not, but we can sure give it a try!"

Emily blushed.

* * * * *

Dear Reader,

It's been nearly seven years since I first "met" the characters in this book. They became my friends over the course of There Comes a Season, my May 1998 release. I can't remember what made me choose their professions, as I'd never personally known either per se, yet two years ago, into my child-care home walked a very special couple. A builder and a doctor, and their son. The Lord truly provides for all of our needs. A month later, the idea for Second Time Around sold, and I began writing Kevin and Emily's story, along with my own "in-house" research team.

I've come to learn that where a door is closed, God often opens a window. I hope you enjoyed reading about the opportunities and second chances facing Kevin and Emily, and how they respond to God's open windows.

As always, I love to hear from my readers. You can write to me at P.O. Box 5021, Greeley, CO 80631-0021.

Carol Steward